Have you g
FAMO

(*Also available as dramatised recordings on CD)

A Note from Enid Blyton's Granddaughter

Welcome to the new edition of The Famous Five series by Enid Blyton. There are 21 books in the collection, a whole world of mystery and adventure to explore. My grandmother, Enid Blyton, wrote her first Famous Five Book, 'Five on a Treasure Island' in 1942. That was in the middle of World War Two (1939–1945). In the story, Julian, Dick and Anne meet their cousin Georgina and her dog, Timmy, for the first time. They soon learn *never* to call her Georgina. Together they explore tunnels and caves, discover hidden passageways and solve crimes.

I first met the Famous Five in a recording of 'Five have a Mystery to Solve'. Julian, Dick, George, Anne and Timmy have developed a love of sausages and can't seem to get enough of them. The sausages are put on hold when a lady knocks at the door of Kirrin Cottage. She has come to ask if the Five could keep her young grandson company in a remote cottage while she is away. The adventure begins as soon as they see the mysterious 'Whispering Island' as they cycle to the cottage to meet the grandson, Wilfred.

Timmy has always been my favourite character. He is the best judge of personality and when he is around, everything seems much safer; not that I am scared of adventure! Since watching the Famous Five television series in the 1970s, which cast Timmy as a Border-Collie sheep dog, I have always wanted to have a Border-Collie.

Who do you think you'll like best?

Sophie Smallwood, 14 June 2010

Five Go To Billycock Hill

Enid Blyton

THE FAMOUS FIVE

Five Go To Billycock Hill

Hodder
Children's
Books

A division of Hachette Children's Books

Copyright © Chorion Rights Ltd
Enid Blyton's signature mark is a Registered Trade Mark of
Chorion Rights Ltd
All rights reserved
'Foreword' copyright Sophie Smallwood 2010

First published in Great Britain in 1956 by Hodder and Stoughton

This revised edition first published in 2010 by Hodder Children's Books

With thanks to Rachel Elliot

The right of Enid Blyton to be identified as the Author of
the Work has been asserted by her in accordance with the
Copyright, Designs and Patents Act 1988.

1

All rights reserved. Apart from any use permitted under UK copyright law,
this publication may only be reproduced, stored or transmitted, in any form,
or by any means with prior permission in writing from the publishers or
in the case of reprographic production in accordance with the terms of
licences issued by the Copyright Licensing Agency and may not be
otherwise circulated in any form of binding or cover other than that in
which it is published and without a similar condition being
imposed on the subsequent purchaser.

All characters in this publication are fictitious and any resemblance
to real persons, living or dead, is purely coincidental.

A Catalogue record for this book is available from the British Library

ISBN 978 0 340 93174 5

Typeset by Avon DataSet Ltd, Bidford-on-Avon, Warwickshire

Printed and bound in Great Britain by Clays Ltd, St Ives plc

The paper and board used in this paperback by Hodder Children's Books
are natural recyclable products made from wood grown in sustainable
forests. The manufacturing processes conform to the environmental
regulations of the country of origin.

Hodder Children's Books
a division of Hachette Children's Books
338 Euston Road, London NW1 3BH
An Hachette UK company
www.hachette.co.uk

Contents

1 A week's holiday

'Where's the map?' said Julian. 'Is that it, George? Good! Now – where shall we spread it?'

'On the floor,' said Anne. 'A map's always easiest to read on the floor. I'll push the table out of the way.'

'Well, be careful, ' said George. 'Dad's in his study, and you know what happened before when someone pushed the table right over!'

Everyone laughed. George's father so often came pouncing out of his study if any sudden noise was made when he was working.

The table was pushed out of the way and the big map unfolded and spread out over the floor. Timmy was surprised to see the four children kneeling down around it, and barked, imagining this was some kind of new game.

'Be quiet, Timmy!' said Dick. 'You've got into trouble once this morning already for making a racket. And stop brushing my face with your tail.'

'Wuff,' said Timmy and lay down heavily on the map.

'Get up,' said Dick. 'Don't you know we're in a hurry? We want to trace our route to Billycock Hill—'

'Billycock Hill – what a lovely name!' said Anne. 'Is that where we're going?'

'Yes,' said Julian, poring over the map. 'It's near some caves we want to see – and there's a butterfly farm not far off, and—'

'A butterfly farm!' said George, surprised. 'Whatever's that?'

'Just what it sounds like!' said Dick. 'A farm for butterflies! Toby, a friend of ours at school, told me about it. He lives quite near it and he says it's a really interesting place – they breed butterflies – and moths, too – from eggs, and sell them to collectors.'

'Do they really?' said Anne. 'I used to enjoy keeping caterpillars and seeing what they turned into – it was like magic to see a lovely butterfly or moth creep out of the chrysalis. But a *farm* for them – can we really go and see it?'

'Oh yes – Toby says the men who run it are very happy to show anyone around,' said Julian.

'Apparently Billycock Hill is a good place for rare butterflies too – that's why they've got their farm there. They rush about with nets half the time – and at night they go moth-hunting.'

'It sounds exciting,' said Dick. 'Well, what with caves to see, and a butterfly farm, and Toby to visit, and—'

'And just Five together again on a sunny week's holiday!' said George, giving Timmy a sudden thump of joy. 'Hurray for half-term and thankfully our two schools had a week's holiday at the same time!'

The four cousins sprawled on the floor, looking with great interest at the map, following out a route with their fingers. As they traced out the way, there came an angry noise from the study, where George's father was at work.

'Who's been tidying my desk? Where are those papers I left here? Fanny, Fanny – come here!'

'He wants Mum – I'll get her,' said George. 'No, I can't – she's gone shopping.'

'Why can't people leave my papers alone?' came her father's voice again. 'Fanny! FANNY!'

Then the study door was flung open and Uncle Quentin came striding out, muttering to himself.

He didn't see the four children on the floor and fell right over them. Timmy barked in delight and leapt at him, thinking that for once George's father was actually having a game with them!

'Oooh!' said George, as her father's hand landed on her face. 'Don't! What are you doing, Dad?'

'Uncle Quentin – sorry you fell over us!' said Julian. 'Shut up, Timmy – this isn't a game!'

He helped his uncle up and waited for the explosion. His uncle brushed himself down and glared at Julian. 'Have you *got* to lie on the floor? Get down, will you, Timmy! Where's your mum, George? Get up, for goodness' sake! Where's Joanna? If she's been tidying my desk again I'll give her her notice!'

Joanna the cook appeared at the doorway, wiping her floury hands on her apron.

'Whatever's all this noise about?' she began. 'Oh sorry – I didn't know it was you. I—'

'Joanna – have you been tidying my desk again?' barked George's father.

'No. Have you lost something? Never you mind, I'll come along and find it,' said Joanna, who was used to his ways. 'Pick up that map, you four – and put the table back. Stop barking, Timmy. George, take him out or your dad will go mad.'

'He's only excited because we're all together again,' said George, and took Timmy into the garden. The others followed, Julian folding up the map, grinning.

'We ought to put Uncle Quentin into a play,' said Dick. 'He'd bring the house down! Well – do we know the way, Julian? And when do we start?'

'Here's Mum,' said George as someone came to the front gate with a basket.

Julian ran to open it. He was very fond of his kindly, pleasant-faced aunt. She smiled round at them all.

'Well – have you decided where to go – and what to take with you? You'll be able to camp out in this beautiful weather – what a lovely half-term it's going to be!'

'Yes,' said Julian, taking his aunt's basket from her and carrying it indoors. 'We're going to Billycock Hill, and as our friend Toby lives at the bottom of it, at Billycock Farm, he's going to lend us all the camping gear we need.'

'So we won't need to load our bikes with tents and camping rolls and things,' said Dick.

'Oh – good!' said his aunt. 'What about food? You can get it at Toby's farm, I suppose?'

'Definitely! We won't *eat* there, of course,' said Julian. 'But we'll buy any eggs or milk or bread we need – and Toby says the strawberries are already ripening!'

Aunt Fanny smiled. 'Well, I needn't worry about your meals, then. And you'll have Timmy with you, too. He'll look after you all, won't you, Timmy? You won't let them get into any trouble, will you?'

'Woof,' said Timmy, in his deepest voice, and wagged his tail. 'Woof.'

'Good old Tim,' said George, patting him. 'If it wasn't for you we'd never be allowed to go off so much on our own, *I* bet!'

'Uncle Quentin's a bit on the warpath, Aunt Fanny,' said Dick. 'He wants to know who's been tidying his desk. He came rushing out of the study, didn't see us lying on the floor round our map – and fell right over us.'

'Oh dear – I'd better go and find out what papers he's lost *now*,' said his aunt. 'I expect he forgot that he had a tidying fit last night, and tidied his desk himself. He's probably put a lot of his most precious papers into the bin!'

Everyone laughed as George's mother hurried into the study.

'Well, let's get ready,' said Julian. 'We won't need to take much, as old Toby's going to help us. Anoraks, of course – and don't forget yours, Timmy! And jumpers. And one or two maps.'

'And torches,' said Anne, 'because we want to explore those caves. Oh, and let's take our swimsuits in *case* we find somewhere to swim. It's warm enough!'

'And candles and matches,' said George, slapping the pocket of her jeans. 'I've got those. I got Joanna to give me three boxes. And let's take some sweets.'

'Yes. That tin of humbugs,' said Julian. 'And I vote we take our little portable radio!'

'Oh yes – that's a good idea,' said Anne, pleased. 'We can hear our favourite programmes then – and the news. I don't suppose we'll be able to buy newspapers.'

'I'll get out the bikes from the shed,' said Julian.

'Dick, get the sandwiches from Joanna – she said she'd make us some because we won't get to Toby's farm till after our dinner-time – and I bet we'll be hungry!'

'Wuff,' said Timmy, who knew that word very well.

'He says remember biscuits for him,' said Anne with a laugh. 'I'll go and get some now, Tim – although I expect you can share meals with the dogs at Billycock Farm.'

Joanna had two large packets of sandwiches and cake ready for them, and two bottles of orangeade.

'There you are,' she said, handing them over. 'And if you get through all those you'll no longer feel hungry. And here are Timmy's biscuits – *and* a bone.'

'You're a star, Joanna,' said Dick, and put his arm round her to give her one of the sudden hugs she liked. 'Well, you'll soon be rid of us – a whole week – isn't that lucky – and with such glorious weather, too.'

'Hurry up!' called Julian. 'I've got the bikes – and no one's had a puncture, for a change. Bring my anorak, Dick.'

In three minutes everything was packed into the bike panniers. Timmy made sure that his biscuits and bone were packed by sniffing at each pack until he came to the smell he was hoping for. Then he wagged his tail and bounded around excitedly. The Five were together again – and who knew what might happen? Timmy was ready for anything!

'Goodbye,' said Mrs Kirrin, standing at the gate to see them go. 'Julian, take care of the others – and Tim, take care of everyone!'

Uncle Quentin suddenly appeared at the window. 'What's all the noise about?' he began impatiently. 'Oh – they're off at last, are they? Now we'll have a little peace and quiet! Goodbye – and behave yourselves!'

'Grown-ups always say that,' said Anne as the Five set off happily, ringing their bells in farewell. 'Hurray – we're off on our own again – yes, you too, Timmy. What fun!'

2 *Off to Billycock Hill*

The sun shone down hotly as the Five sped down the sandy road that ran alongside Kirrin Bay. Timmy loped easily beside them, his tongue hanging out quite a long way. Anne always said that he had the longest tongue of any dog she had ever known!

The sea was as blue as forget-me-nots as they cycled along beside it. Across the bay they could see little Kirrin Island, with Kirrin Castle towering up.

'Doesn't it look wonderful?' said Dick. 'I half wish we were going to spend half-term at Kirrin Cottage, and were going swimming, and rowing across to George's little island over there.'

'We can do that in the summer holidays,' said Julian. 'It's fun to explore other parts of the country when we can. Toby says the caves in Billycock Hill are amazing.'

'What's Toby like?' asked George. 'We've never

seen him, Anne and I.'

'He's a bit of a joker,' said Dick. 'Likes to put caterpillars down people's necks and so on – and beware if he has a beautiful rose in his buttonhole and asks you to smell it.'

'Why?' asked Anne, surprised.

'Because when you bend down to smell it you'll get a squirt of water in your face,' said Dick. 'It's a trick rose.'

'I don't think I'm going to like him much,' said George, who didn't take kindly to tricks of this sort. 'I'll probably bash him on the head if he does things like that to me.'

'That won't be any good,' said Dick cheerfully. 'He won't bash you back – he'll just think up some worse trick. Don't scowl, George – we're on holiday! Toby's all right – a bit of a joker, that's all.'

They had now left Kirrin Bay behind and were cycling down a country lane, set with hawthorn hedges each side. May was over now, and the first wild roses were showing pink here and there. A little breeze got up, and was very welcome indeed.

'We'll have an ice-cream when we come to a

village,' said Julian after they had cycled about six miles.

'*Two* ice-creams,' said Anne. 'Oh dear – this hill – what a steep one we've come to. I don't know whether it's worse to ride up slowly and painfully, or to get off and push my bike to the top.'

Timmy tore up to the top in front of them and then sat down to wait in the cool breeze there, his tongue hanging out longer than ever. Julian came to the top first and looked down the other side.

'There's a village there,' he said. 'Right at the bottom. Let's see – yes, it's Tennick village – we'll stop and ask if it sells ice-creams.'

It did, of course – strawberry and vanilla. The four children sat on a seat under a tree outside the small village shop, and dug little wooden spoons into ice-cream tubs. Timmy sat nearby, watching hopefully. He knew that at least he would be able to lick out the empty tubs.

'Oh, Tim – I didn't mean to buy you one, because you really are a bit fat,' said George, looking at the beseeching brown eyes fixed on her ice-cream. 'But as you'll probably get very thin running so far while we're cycling, I'll buy you a whole one for yourself.'

'Wuff,' said Timmy, bounding into the little shop at once and putting his great paws up on the counter, much to the surprise of the woman behind it.

'It's a waste, really, giving Timmy an ice-cream,' said Anne when George and the dog came out. 'He just loosens it with his tongue and gulps it down. I sometimes wonder he doesn't chew up the cardboard tub, too!'

After ten minutes' rest they all set off again, feeling nice and cool inside. It really was lovely cycling through the June countryside – the trees were so fresh and green still, and the fields they passed were golden with buttercups – thousands and thousands of them, nodding their polished heads in the wind.

There was very little traffic on these deserted country roads – an occasional farm-vehicle, and sometimes a car, but little else. The Five kept to the lanes as much as they could, for they all preferred their winding curves set with hedges of all kinds to the wide, dusty main roads, straight and uninteresting.

'We ought to get to Billycock Farm about four

o'clock,' said Dick. 'Or maybe sooner. What time do we have our lunch, Julian? And where?'

'We'll find a good place about one o'clock,' said Julian. 'And not a minute before. So it's no good anyone saying they're hungry yet. It's only twelve.'

'I'm more thirsty than hungry,' said Anne. 'And I'm sure Timmy must be dying of thirst! Let's stop at the next stream so that he can have a drink.'

'There's one,' said Dick, pointing to where a stream wound across a nearby field. 'Hey, Tim – go and have a drink!'

Timmy shot through the hedge to the stream and began to lap. The others dismounted and stood waiting. Anne picked a spray of honeysuckle and put it through a buttonhole of her blouse. 'Now I can sniff it all the time,' she said. 'Delicious!'

'Hey, Tim – leave some water for the fishes!' shouted Dick. 'George, stop him drinking any more. He's swelling up like a balloon.'

'He's *not*,' said George. 'Timmy! That's enough! Here, boy, here!'

Timmy took one last lap and then raced over to George. He pranced round her, barking joyfully.

'There – he feels much better now,' said George, and away they all went again, groaning as they cycled slowly up the many hills in that part of the country, and shouting with delight as they sped furiously down the other side.

Julian had decided where to have their midday meal – on the top of a high hill! Then they could see all the country for miles around, and there would also be a nice cooling breeze.

'Cheer up,' he said as they came to the steepest hill they had so far encountered. 'We'll have our lunch at the top of this hill – and a good long rest!'

'At last!' panted Anne. 'We'll be aching all over tomorrow!'

It really was lovely at the top of the hill! It was so high that they could see the countryside spreading for miles and miles around them.

'You can see five counties from here,' said Julian. 'But don't ask me which – I've forgotten! Let's lie in this heather and have a bit of a rest before we have our lunch.'

It was soft and comfortable lying in the springy heather, but Timmy did not approve of a rest before lunch. He wanted his bone! He went to where George had put her bike down, and sniffed in her carrier. Yes – his bone was definitely there! He glanced around to make sure that everyone was resting, and nobody watching him. Then he began to nuzzle a paper parcel.

Anne was lying nearest to him, and she heard the crackling of the paper and sat up. '*Timmy*!' she said, shocked. 'Oh, Timmy – fancy helping yourself to our sandwiches!'

George sat up at once, and Timmy put his tail down, still wagging it a little as if to say, 'Sorry – but after all, it *is* my bone!'

'Oh – he just wants his bone,' said George. 'He's not after our sandwiches. As if he *would* take them, Anne! You might have known he wouldn't!'

'I feel rather like having mine now,' said Anne. 'Julian, can't we have some? – and I *really* want a drink.'

The idea of a drink made everyone long to begin lunch and soon they were unwrapping ham-and-tomato sandwiches, and enormous slices of Joanna's fruitcake. Julian found the little cardboard drinking cups, and poured out the orangeade carefully.

'This is great,' said Dick, munching his sandwiches and gazing out over the rolling countryside, with its moorlands, its stretches of farmland with the fields of green corn, and its sloping hills. 'Look – see that hill far away in the distance, Julian – over there – would that be Billycock Hill, do you think? It's rather a funny shape.'

'I'll look through my binoculars,' said Julian, and took them from their leather case. He put them to his eyes and stared hard at the faraway hill that lay to the north of them.

'Yes – I think it probably is Billycock Hill,' he said. 'It's got such an odd-shaped top; it looks a bit like an old Billycock bowler hat.'

He handed the binoculars round, and everyone looked at the far-off hill. George put the binoculars to Timmy's eyes. 'There you are!' she said. 'Have a look, Timmy! Julian, it doesn't look so very far away.'

'It's not, as the crow flies,' said Julian, taking back his binoculars and surveying the countryside around them again. 'But it's a long, long way through those hundreds of little winding lanes. Any more sandwiches, anyone?'

'There aren't any more left,' said Dick. 'Or fruitcake either. Have a humbug if you're still hungry.'

The humbugs were passed round and Timmy waited hopefully for his turn. George gave him one. 'Not that it's much use to you,' she said. 'You just swallow it without even one suck!'

'We'll rest for half an hour more,' said Julian. 'Oh, I'm so sleepy!'

They all snuggled down into the soft clumps of heather, and soon they were asleep in the warm sun. Even Timmy snoozed, with one ear half up just in case someone came by. But nobody did. In fact it was so very quiet on the top of the hill that three-quarters of an hour went by before anyone awoke. Anne felt something crawling up her arm and woke with a jump.

'Ugh – a big beetle!' she said, and shook it off. She glanced at her watch. 'Dick! Ju! Wake up! We must get on, or we'll never be there by tea-time!'

Soon they were once more on their way, tearing down the hill at top speed, shouting as they went, with Timmy barking madly beside them. Really, the start of a holiday was the happiest thing in the world!

3 Billycock Farm

The Five cycled fast that afternoon, and would have arrived at Billycock Hill even sooner than they did if it hadn't been for Timmy. He panted so much in the heat that they stopped for brief rests every fifteen minutes.

'It's a pity he's so big and heavy,' said Anne. 'If he'd been a small dog we could have taken turns at carrying him on our bikes.'

Billycock Hill was soon very near. It certainly was a strange shape, very like an old-fashioned bowler hat. It was partly heather-clad and partly sloping meadow land. Cows grazed in the meadows, and farther up the hill, where there was shorter, wiry grass, the farmer had put a good many sheep.

Nestling down at the foot of the hill was a rambling old farm building, with outhouses and stables and a big greenhouse.

'That must be Billycock Farm,' said Julian.

'Well, we've made very good time, you know – it's only half past three. Let's wash our faces in that stream over there – we all look rather hot and dirty. Timmy, you can have a swim if you want to!'

The water was cool and silky to the touch, and the children splashed it over their faces and necks, wishing they could do as Timmy was doing – lying down in the stream and letting the water flow over him!

'That's better,' said Dick, mopping his face with an enormous handkerchief. 'Now let's go and present ourselves at Billycock Farm. I hope Toby's remembered that we're coming – he *promised* to lend us all we wanted for camping out.'

They combed their hair, brushed down their clothes with their hands, and then, feeling more respectable, made their way across a field-path to a farm gate. The field was bumpy, so they rode slowly.

Soon they were in a big farmyard, with hens pecking around them, and ducks swimming on a round duck-pond. Farm dogs began barking from somewhere – and then something ran round the corner of the old house – something very small and pink.

'Whatever is it?' said Anne. 'Oh – it's a piglet! What a pet! Oh, it's come right up to us – little piglet, have you escaped from your sty? How clean you are!'

The tiny pig gave funny little squeals, and ran up to Timmy, who sat back on his haunches in surprise, staring at this unexpected little creature. He thought it must be some sort of dog without any hair.

The piglet butted Timmy gently and Timmy retreated backwards. Julian laughed. 'Tim can't make it out!' he said. 'No don't growl, Timmy – it's harmless!'

'Look – who's this?' said Dick as a small figure came round the house. It stopped when it saw the Five.

'What a sweet little boy!' said Anne. 'Is he Toby's brother?'

The child didn't look more than five years old. He had a head of bright yellow curls, big brown eyes, and a grin just like his big brother's.

'That's my pig,' he said, coming slowly towards them. 'He runned away from me.'

Anne laughed. 'What's your pig's name?' she said.

'Curly,' said the small boy, and pointed at the piglet's tail. 'He's got a curly tail. It won't go straight.'

'It's a nice tail,' said Anne.

The piglet ran to the small boy, and he grabbed it by its tail. 'You runned away again,' he said. Then he picked up the pig and walked off.

'Hey! Is this Billycock Farm?' called Julian. 'Have you got a brother called Toby?'

'Toby? Yes, Toby's over there,' said the boy, and he pointed to a big barn. 'Toby's ratting with Binky.'

'Right,' said Julian. The little boy disappeared with his funny pet, and Julian laughed. 'Come on – let's go and find Toby and Binky. Perhaps Binky's another brother.'

'Or a dog,' said George, and put her hand on Timmy's collar. 'Better be careful. He might go for Tim.'

'Yes – Binky might be a dog, of course – probably a good ratter,' said Julian. 'Dick and I will go to the barn and you two stay here with Timmy.'

They went off to the barn. A great noise came from inside as the two boys approached.

Shouts and barks and the rap of a stick came to their ears.

'Get him, Binky – look, he went under that sack! Oh, you silly, you've lost him again!'

Wuff-wuff-wuff! Rap-rap! More yells! In great curiosity Julian and Dick peered into the rather dark old barn. They saw Toby there, prodding under sacks, with a very excited collie beside him, barking incessantly.

'Hey, Toby!' yelled Julian, and Toby stood up and turned a red and perspiring face towards the two boys.

'Oh – you've arrived!' he said, going quickly to the door. 'I thought you were never coming. Glad to see you! But are there only two of you? I got out tents and things for four.'

'There *are* four of us – five counting Timmy,' said Julian. 'We've left the two girls over there with him – he's our dog. Will yours be friendly or not?'

'Oh, yes, as long as I introduce them,' said Toby and they all went out of the barn. As soon as Binky, Toby's dog, saw Timmy, he stood still, made himself stiff and growled, while the hackles on his neck slowly rose up.

'It's all right,' shouted Toby to the girls. 'Bring your dog here. He'll be all right with Binky in half a minute.'

Rather doubtfully George brought Timmy across. Timmy was a bit doubtful himself of this big collie! Toby bent down and spoke into Binky's ear.

'Binky, shake paws with this nice girl – she's a friend.' He nodded at George. 'Hold out your hand,' he said.

George bent down to the collie and held out her hand. At once the dog put up his paw and allowed her to shake it solemnly.

'Now you,' said Toby to Anne, and she did the same. She liked this dog Binky, with his bright brown eyes and long, sleek nose.

'Does *your* dog shake hands, too?' asked Toby. George nodded. 'He does? Right – tell him to shake paws with Binky. Binky, shake!'

'Timmy, shake,' commanded George, and very politely and solemnly the two dogs shook paws, eyeing each other cautiously. Timmy gave a sudden little whine – and then the two were tearing round the yard together, barking furiously, chasing one another, rolling over, and having a wonderful game.

'That's all right, then,' said Toby, pleased. 'Binky's all right with anyone, human or animal, as long as he can shake hands with them. I've taught him that. But he's a useless ratter! He just can't seem to nip a rat. Well – let's go and see my mum. She's expecting you. She's got a whopping great tea.'

This was all very satisfactory! Just the kind of welcome the Five liked. Anne looked sideways at Toby. She thought he was nice. George wasn't so sure. He had a rose in his buttonhole – was it a trick one, and was he going to ask her to smell it?

'We saw a little yellow-haired boy just now,' said Anne. 'With a tiny piglet.'

'Oh, that's Benny with his pet pig,' said Toby, laughing. 'He calls it Curly – and he adores it! We've offered him a kitten or a puppy – but no, he wants that piglet. They go everywhere together – like Mary and her lamb! Benny's a pet – he really is. Kid brothers are usually a nuisance, you know, but Benny isn't.'

'Kid sisters are a bit of a nuisance sometimes too,' said Dick, glancing slyly at Anne, who at once gave him a determined punch. 'Still – Anne's not too bad, is she, Ju?'

Toby's mother, Mrs Thomas, was a plump and cheerful woman, with a smile as wide as Toby's and Benny's. She made them all very welcome.

'Come along in,' she said. 'Toby's pleased you're going to camp around here – he's got all the tents and rugs you'll need – and you can come every day and get eggs and milk and bread and butter and anything else you need from here. Don't be afraid to ask!'

There was suddenly the scamper of little hooves and Curly the piglet came running indoors.

'There, now!' said Toby's mother. 'There's that piglet again. Benny, Benny – you are NOT to let Curly come indoors. Cats I don't mind, nor dogs – but pigs I won't have. Benny!'

Benny appeared, looking very apologetic. 'Sorry, Mum – but he's lively today. Oooh, what a tea! Can we have some yet?'

'I'll just make the tea – unless you'd rather have some of our creamy milk?' said Toby's mother.

'Oh, milk, please, Mrs Thomas,' said Anne, and they all said the same. Nothing could be nicer than icy-cold, creamy farm milk from the dairy on a hot day like this.

They all sat down to tea, and the four visitors wished they hadn't had such a big lunch! A large ham sat on the table, and there were crusty loaves of new bread. Crisp lettuces, dewy and cool, and red radishes were side by side in a big glass dish. On the sideboard was an enormous cake, and beside it a dish of scones. Great slabs of butter and jugs of creamy milk were there, too, with honey and home-made jam.

'I wish I was hungry, *really* hungry,' said Dick. 'This is just the kind of meal for a hungry day.'

'I didn't think you'd have had much lunch,' said Mrs Thomas. 'Now then, Toby – you're the host. See to your guests, please – and, Benny, take the piglet off your knee. I will *not* have him at the table.'

'Curly will be very upset if he sees that ham,' said Toby slyly. 'That's his grandfather!'

Benny put Curly down hurriedly, afraid that his feelings might be hurt. The piglet went to sit beside Timmy, who, very much surprised, but rather pleased, at once made room for him.

It was a very happy meal, and Toby was a good host. Anne sat beside little Benny, and found herself liking him more than ever. 'He's like a little boy out of a story,' she said to George. 'He and Curly ought to be put into a book!'

'Well now,' said Mrs Thomas after everyone had eaten their fill, 'what are your plans? Toby, show them where you've put their tents and everything. Then they can decide where they're going to camp.'

'Come on, then,' said Toby, and Benny and Curly and Binky all came along, too. 'You can help to carry everything – and we'll go up on Billycock Hill and find a good camping place. I wish I could camp out with you too!'

Away they all went, feeling rather full but very happy. Where should they camp? How lovely to sleep out at nights, and see the stars through the opening in the tent!

4 *A wonderful camping place*

Toby had put all the camping gear in a nearby barn. He took the Five there, with Benny and the piglet trailing after. Binky came, too, so friendly now with Timmy that they trotted along side by side, occasionally pushing against each other like schoolboys!

They all looked at the pile of canvas, the pegs and the ropes. Yes, these two tents would do very well, although if the weather stayed like this they would hardly need tents! They could lay their rugs out on the springy heather.

'This is wonderful, Toby,' said Julian gratefully. 'You've even given us a kettle and a frying pan.'

'Well, you might want to cook a meal,' said Toby. 'Or boil soup. There's a saucepan for that – ah, here it is!'

He picked it up and promptly put it on Benny's head, where it stuck tightly on his yellow curls. Benny yelled and ran at Toby, hitting him with his fists. The little pig rushed away in fright and disappeared round a corner.

Anne took the saucepan off poor Benny's head. 'You're all right!' she said. 'It was a funny hat to wear, wasn't it?'

'Curly runned away again!' wept Benny, and he pummelled the laughing Toby. 'I hate you, I hate you!'

'You go and find him,' said Toby, fending off the angry small boy, and Benny ran off on his fat little legs.

'Well, we've got rid of him for a few minutes,' said Toby. 'Now – is there anything I've forgotten? You've got torches, I suppose? What about candles – and matches?'

'We've got those, too,' said Dick. 'And we've brought jumpers and swimsuits – but that's about all. I see you've put a couple of rugs here as well in case we're cold!'

'Well, it *might* turn wet and chilly,' said Toby. 'Of course, if it snows, or anything like that, you'll have to come and borrow some more rugs! Now, shall I help you to fix them on your bikes?'

It was too difficult to fix anything on to the

four bikes, and in the end Toby found a handcart and the children piled everything into that.

'We'll fetch our bikes some other time,' said Julian.

'Leave them here!' said Toby. 'They'll be all right. Are you going now? Well, I'll get a package Mum's got ready for you – you know, ham and new-laid eggs and bread and butter and the rest.'

'It's really good of her,' said Julian gratefully. 'Well, let's start – we've got everything in the handcart now. We'll just wait for the food. Dick, you and I can push this handcart together. It'll need two of us up the hill – and I vote we camp on the side of the slope somewhere, so that we can get a good view.'

Toby came back with an enormous package of food. Benny came with him, Curly trotting behind. Benny carried a basket of ripe strawberries.

'I picked them for you,' he said, and handed them to Anne.

'What beauties!' she said, and gave the smiling child a hug. 'We'll enjoy them, Benny.'

'Can I come and see your camp when you've

built it?' he asked. 'Can I bring Curly? He's never seen a camp.'

'Yes, of course you can,' said Anne. 'Are we ready now, Julian? What about milk? Mrs Thomas said we could take some.'

'Oh yes – I forgot that,' said Toby. 'It's in the dairy.'

He sped off with Binky, and the others arranged everything neatly in the useful little handcart. Toby came back with the milk – two big bottles. They were stacked carefully in a corner of the cart.

'Well, we're ready now, I think,' said Julian, and he and Dick began to push the cart down the path to the gate. Timmy and Binky trotted on ahead, and everyone else followed. Benny came as far as the gate with Curly, then Toby sent him back.

'You know what Mum said, Benny,' he said. 'You're not to come with us now – it'll be too late when Binky and I come back.'

Benny's mouth went down, but he didn't attempt to follow them. He picked Curly up in his arms in case the piglet ran after the others.

'Benny's sweet,' said Anne. 'I wish I had a

little brother like that.'

'He's all right,' said Toby. 'A bit of a cry-baby, though. I'm *trying* to bring him up properly – teasing him out of his babyishness, and making him stand on his own feet.'

'He seems to be able to do that all right,' said Dick. 'The way he went for you when you put that saucepan on his head! He pummelled you right and left!'

'Benny's a funny little kid,' said Toby, giving a hand with the cart as they reached the slope of the hill. 'He's always having funny pets. Two years ago he had a lamb that followed him everywhere. Last year he had two goslings that followed him about – and when they grew into geese they still followed him! They waddled all the way upstairs one day!'

'And this year he's got a pig!' said George, who, like Anne, was very very amused by Benny. 'Don't you think Timmy was very funny with Curly? I'm sure he still thinks it's a puppy without any hair!'

They made their way up the hill, following a narrow sheep-path. The handcart bumped and wobbled, and soon it needed four or five pairs of hands to push it.

'How much farther?' panted Toby at last. 'Surely you're not going right to the top?'

'No,' said Julian. 'About halfway up. We do want to have a good view, Toby. Not very much farther up, I should think. But let's have a bit of rest, shall we?'

They sat down, glad to get their breath. The view was magnificent. Far away on the horizon were purplish hills, and in front of them stretched miles and miles of green and golden countryside. Green for growing corn and grass – gold for the buttercups, which were at their best in this sunny week of June.

'I like those silvery threads here and there winding about the green fields,' said Anne. 'Little streams – or rivers – curving like snakes all about! And I like the dark green patches that are woods.'

'What's that just down there?' asked George, pointing to what looked like an enormous field with great sheds in the centre.

'That's an airfield,' said Toby promptly. 'A bit hush-hush. Secret planes tried out, and all that. I know all about it because a cousin of mine is there – he's a flight-lieutenant. He comes to see us sometimes and tells me things. It's an experimental place.'

'What's that, exactly?' asked Anne.

'Well – where new ideas are tried out,' said Toby. 'They deal mostly with very small planes down there – one-man fighter planes, I think. Don't be scared if you hear noises from the airfield sometimes – bangs and bursts. I don't know what they are, of course – it's all to do with their experiments.'

'I wish I could visit the airfield,' said Dick. 'I'm keen on planes. I'm going to fly one when I'm older.'

'You'd better meet my cousin, then,' said Toby. 'He might take you up in one.'

'I'd *really* like to meet him,' said Dick, delighted. 'So would Julian.'

'We'd better get on now,' said Julian, standing up. 'We won't go much higher – the view can't be much better anywhere else!'

George and Anne went on ahead to find a good camping place, while the three boys pushed the cart slowly over the heather. But it was Timmy who found the right place! He ran on ahead, feeling thirsty, so when he heard the sound of running water he ran to it at once.

From under a jutting rock gushed a little spring. It rippled down a rocky shelf and lost itself in a mass of lush greenery below. Rushes grew to mark the way it went, and George's sharp eyes could follow its path for quite a long way down the hill, outlined by the dark line of rushes.

'Julian! Look what Timmy's found!' she called as she watched him lap from the clear spring water. 'A little spring gushing out of the hillside! Hadn't we better camp near it?'

'Good idea!' shouted back Julian, and left the handcart to come and see. 'Yes, this is just the place! A great view – plenty of springy heather to camp on – and water laid on quite near!'

Everyone agreed that it was a wonderful place, and soon all the gear was taken from the handcart. The tents were not erected, for everyone meant to sleep under the stars that night, the evening was so warm. Nobody wanted to lie in a stuffy tent!

Anne unpacked the food parcel, wondering where would be the coolest place for a 'larder'. She went over to the rock from which gushed the crystal-clear spring water. She pushed away the rushes around and discovered a kind of small cave hollowed out of the rock below the spring.

'It'd be as cool as anything in there,' thought Anne, and put her hand through the falling water into the cave-like hole. Yes, it was icy cold! Was it big enough to hold the milk bottles and everything? Just about, she thought.

Anne loved arranging anything, and she was soon at work putting away the food and the milk into her odd larder. George laughed when she saw it.

'Just like you, Anne!' she said. 'Well, we'd better put a towel by the spring, for we'll get soaked every time we get out any food!'

'Tell Timmy he's *not* to try and poke his head into my larder,' said Anne, pushing Timmy away. 'Oh, now he's all wet. Go and shake yourself somewhere else, Timmy – you're showering me with drops of water!'

Toby had to leave them, for it was already past his supper-time. 'See you tomorrow!' he said. 'I wish I was staying up here with you! Bye!'

Away he went down the hill with Binky

at his heels. The Five looked at one another and grinned.

'He's nice – but it's good to be alone again – just us Five,' said George. 'Come on – let's settle in. This is the best camp we've ever had!'

5 The first night – and a morning visitor

'What's the time?' said Julian, looking at his watch. 'Oh! – it's almost eight o'clock. Anyone feel tired?'

'Yes,' said Dick, Anne and George, and even Timmy joined in with his deepest 'Woof'.

'With all that bicycling and then pushing that heavy cart up the hill, I can hardly move!' said Dick. 'I vote we have a simple supper – something out of Anne's little larder – and then spread our rugs over some thick heather and sleep under the sky. Even up here, with a breeze, it's warm. I'd be stifled in a tent.'

'Well, we're all agreed on that,' said Julian. 'Anne, what do you suggest for a light supper?'

'Bread, butter and some of Mrs Thomas's farm cheese,' said Anne promptly. 'With a tomato or two if you like and icy cold milk and Benny's strawberries to finish with. That is – if the milk has had time to get cold in the little hole under the spring.'

'Sounds really good,' said Julian. 'What do *you* think, Timmy? Anne, if you and George get the supper ready, Dick and I will prepare our heathery beds. Then we can all go to sleep as soon as possible. I honestly feel that once I sit down or lie down I won't be able to get up again!'

'Same here,' said Dick, and went off with Julian to find the best place for sleeping. They soon found one. They came across a giant of a gorse bush, thick, prickly and still full of golden blooms. In front of it was a stretch of very close-set heather, as springy as the best mattress in the world. Dick sat down on it and grinned at Julian.

'Just made for us!' he said. 'We'll sleep like logs here. We hardly need a rug to lie on, it's so close-grown. Help me up – legs won't do anything now I've sat down!'

Julian pulled him up and they called to the girls: 'Anne! George! Bring the supper here. We've found a good place. It's by this giant gorse bush.'

The girls came along with the meal, and the boys fetched a couple of rugs from the pile of things that they had brought in the handcart.

They spread them on the heather.

'This is a really good place,' said George, coming up with Anne and Timmy carrying a loaf of bread, a pat of butter and tomatoes. Anne had the milk and the cheese. Timmy was carrying a little bag of his own biscuits.

'The gorse bush will shelter us from too much wind,' said Dick, taking the milk from Anne. 'It's an ideal spot – and the view is amazing.'

It was a very happy supper they had, sitting in the heather, while the sun sank lower and lower in the west. The evenings were very light now, and they wouldn't need candles! They ate up everything, and then went to wash at the little spring that bubbled out so cheerfully.

They lay down on their rugs in the heather while it was still daylight. 'Goodnight!' said Dick, and promptly fell fast asleep. 'Goodnight!' called Julian and lay for a few seconds looking at the view, which was now becoming dim and blue.

Timmy kept the two girls awake for a minute or two, trying to squeeze in between them. 'Please keep still, Timmy,' said George. 'And just remember you're on guard, even though I don't expect there's anyone nearer than a mile – and that'll be at Billycock Farm! Lie still now, or I'll push you off the rug! Goodnight, Anne.'

George was soon asleep, and so was Timmy, tired out with so many miles of running. Anne lay awake for a few minutes, looking at the evening star which shone large and golden in the sky. She felt very happy. 'I don't want to grow up,' she thought. 'There can't be anything nicer in the world than this – being with the others, having fun with them. No – I don't want to grow up!'

Then she, too, fell asleep, and night came quietly down, with stars brilliant in the sky, and very little noise to be heard anywhere – just the gurgling of the spring some way away, and the far-off bark of some dog – perhaps Binky at the farm. The breeze died down, so that even that could not be heard.

No one except Timmy awoke at all that night. Timmy put up one ear when he heard a squeak just above his head. It came again and he opened one eye. It was a small black bat circling and swooping, hunting for insects. Its squeak was so high that only Timmy's quick ear caught it. He put down his listening ear and went to sleep again.

Nobody stirred until a very loud noise awakened them. R-r-r-r-r-r-r-r-r! R-r-r-r-r-r-r-r-r-r! They all woke up with a jump and the boys sat up straight, startled. What could it be?

'It's a plane,' said Julian, staring up at a small aeroplane flying over the hill. 'It must be one from that airfield down there! Hey – it's five past nine! Five past nine – we've slept for nearly twelve hours!'

'Well, I'm going to sleep for some more,' said Dick, snuggling down into his heathery bed again and shutting his eyes.

'No, you're not,' said Julian, giving him a shove. 'It's too good a day to waste in any more sleep. Hey, you girls – are you awake?'

'Yes,' called George, sitting up, rubbing her eyes. 'That aeroplane woke me. Anne's awake, too – and you can see that Timmy is; he's gone after a rabbit or something.'

'We'll go and wash at the spring,' said Anne, scrambling off the rug. 'And then we'll get breakfast. Anyone like a boiled egg?'

The sun shone down out of a blue sky, and the little breeze awoke and began to blow again. They washed in the cold water, and Timmy drank it, lapping it thirstily as it splashed down over his nose. Then they had their breakfast.

It was easy to make a little fire in the shelter of the giant gorse bush, and boil the eggs in the saucepan. Bread and butter and tomatoes completed the simple meal, with cold creamy milk to wash it down.

In the middle of this Timmy began to bark frantically, but as his tail was wagging all the time, the others guessed that it must be Toby coming. They heard Binky's answering bark, and then the dog himself appeared, panting and excited. He greeted Timmy first of all, and then ran round to give everyone a lick.

'Hello, hello, hello!' came Toby's voice, and he appeared round the gorse bush. 'Had a good night? Hey, aren't you late – *still* having your breakfast? You sleepyheads! I've been up since six. I've milked cows and cleaned out a shed, and fed the hens and collected the eggs.'

The Five immediately felt ashamed of themselves! They gazed at Toby in admiration – he was a proper farmer!

'I've brought you some more milk, bread and eggs and cake,' he said, and put down a basket.

'That's really good of you,' said Julian. 'We must pay for any food we get from your farm, you know that. Any idea of how much we owe for yesterday's food and for what you've brought today?'

'Well, my mum says you don't *need* to pay her,' said Toby. 'But I know you want to – so how about you pay *me* each time and I'll put the money into a box and buy my mum a fantastic present at the end – from you all. Will that do?'

'That's a good idea,' said Julian. 'We couldn't possibly accept food if we didn't pay for it – but I know what mums are – they don't like being paid in money for their kindness! So we'll do what you say. Now, reckon up what we owe so far, and I'll pay you.'

'Right,' said Toby in a businesslike way. 'I'll charge you market prices, not top prices. I'll just tot up the bill while you're clearing up and putting away what I've brought.'

Dick and Anne washed up in the spring, and Julian and George carried everything there to put in their 'larder'. Toby presented Julian with a neatly written bill, which he at once paid. Toby receipted the bill and gave it back.

'There you are – all businesslike,' he said. 'Thanks very much. What are you going to do today? There are wonderful caves to be explored if you like – or there's the butterfly farm – or you can just come down to *our* farm for the day.'

'No, not today,' said Julian, afraid that they might make themselves a nuisance to Mrs Thomas. 'I don't feel like seeing caves this morning either – so dark and eerie on such a sunny day. What shall we do, girls?'

But before they could decide Binky and Timmy began to bark, each dog standing completely still, facing the same way – towards the giant gorse bush.

'Who is it, Tim?' asked George. 'Go and see! Go on then!'

Timmy ran behind the bush, followed by Binky, and then the children heard a surprised voice.

'Hello, Binky! What are *you* doing all the way up here? And who's your friend?'

'It's Mr Gringle,' said Toby. 'One of the men who own the butterfly farm. He's often up here with his net, because it's a wonderful place for butterflies.'

A man came round the gorse bush – rather a

strange figure, untidy, with glasses slipping down his nose, and his hair much too long. He carried a big butterfly net and stopped when he saw the five children.

'Hello!' he said. 'Who are all these, Toby? Quite a crowd!'

'Friends of mine, Mr Gringle,' said Toby solemnly. 'Allow me to introduce them. Julian Kirrin, Dick Kirrin, Anne Kirrin, George Kirrin, their cousin – and their dog Timothy.'

'Ha – pleased to meet you!' said Mr Gringle, and came shambling forward, his big butterfly net over his shoulder. Behind his glasses shone curiously bright eyes. He nodded his head to each of the four cousins. 'Three boys – and a girl. Very nice lot, too. You don't look as if you'll leave litter about or start fires in this lovely countryside.'

'We wouldn't dream of it,' said George, delighted that he'd thought she was a boy. Nothing pleased George as much as that! 'Mr Gringle – *could* we see your butterfly farm, please? We'd really like to!'

'Of course, my dear boy, of course,' said Mr Gringle, and his eyes shone as if he were pleased.

6 *The butterfly farm*

Mr Gringle led the way down the hill by a little path so overgrown that it was hardly possible to see it. Halfway down the little company heard a squealing noise – and then an excited little voice.

'Toby, Toby! I'm here! Can I come with you?'

'It's Benny – and the piglet!' said Anne, amused at the little couple making their way excitedly towards them.

Timmy ran to Curly and sniffed him all over, still not quite sure that he wasn't some kind of strange puppy.

'What are you doing up here?' said Toby sternly. 'You know you're not supposed to wander too far from the farm. You'll get lost one of these days, Benny.'

'Curly runned away,' said Benny, looking up at his big brother with wide brown eyes.

'You mean you wanted to find out where

I'd gone so you came after me with Curly,' said Toby.

'Curly runned away, he runned fast!' said Benny, looking as if he was going to cry.

'You're a rascal, Benny,' said Toby. 'You make that piglet of yours an excuse for getting about all over the place. You wait till Dad hears it – you'll get such a telling off. Well – tag along with us now – we're going to the butterfly farm. And if Curly runs away, let him! I'm tired of that pig.'

'I'll carry him,' said Benny, and picked up the little creature in his arms. But he soon had to put him down, for Curly squealed so loudly that Timmy and Binky both leapt round him in great concern.

'Hmm – well – shall we proceed?' asked Mr Gringle, walking on in front. 'Quite a party we have today.'

'Are your butterflies afraid of pigs or dogs?' asked Benny, trotting beside him. 'Shall we leave them outside?'

'Don't ask idiotic questions, Benny,' said Toby. Then he gave a cry and caught Mr Gringle's arm. 'Hey – look at that butterfly. Don't you want to catch it? Is it rare?'

'No,' said Mr Gringle rather coldly. 'It's a Meadow-Brown – very common indeed. Don't they teach you anything at school? Fancy not knowing that!'

'Julian, do we have any butterfly lessons?' asked Toby with a grin. 'Mr Gringle, what about you coming and teaching us about Cabbage butterflies and Cauliflower moths, and Red Admirals and Blue Captains and Peacock butterflies and Ostrich moths and—'

'Don't be silly, Toby,' said Julian, seeing that Mr Gringle had no sense of humour at all, and didn't think this at all funny. 'Mr Gringle, are there many rare butterflies around here?'

'Oh, yes, yes,' said the butterfly man. 'But not only that – there are so many of *all* kinds here, and it's easy to catch as many as I want for breeding purposes. One butterfly means hundreds of eggs, you know – and we hatch them out and sell them.'

He suddenly made a dart to one side, almost knocking George over. 'Sorry, boy!' he said, making the others smile. 'Sorry! There's a Brown Argus there – a lovely specimen, first I've seen this year! Stand clear, will you.'

The children – and the dogs too – stood still as he tiptoed towards a small dark brown butterfly spreading its tiny wings as it sat on a flowering plant. With a swift downwards swoop the net closed over the plant, and in a flash the butterfly man had caught the fluttering insect. He pinched the net inwards, and showed the children the tiny creature.

'There you are – a female Brown Argus, one of the family of the Blue butterflies you see so often in full summer. She'll lay me plenty of eggs and they'll all hatch into fat little slug-like caterpillars, and—'

'But this isn't a blue butterfly,' said Anne, looking through the fine net. 'It's dark brown, with a row of pretty orange spots along the margins of its wings.'

'All the same, it belongs to the Blue butterfly family,' said Mr Gringle, taking it out with the gentlest of fingers and putting it into a tin case slung round his shoulders. 'It's probably come up from one of those hay meadows down in the valley there. In you go, my little beauty!'

'Mr Gringle, quick – here's a lovely butterfly!'

called George. 'It's got greeny-black front wings with red spots, and lovely red back wings with dark green borders. Oh, quick – I'm sure you want this one!'

'That's not a butterfly,' said Dick, who knew a lot about them.

'I should think not!' said Mr Gringle, getting his net poised ready to swoop. 'It's a moth – a lovely little thing!' Down went his net and the pretty little red-and-green insect fluttered in surprise inside it.

'But moths don't fly in the daytime,' argued George. 'Only at night.'

'Rubbish!' said Mr Gringle, looking at the moth through the thick lenses of his glasses. 'What are boys coming to nowadays? In *my* boyhood nearly every boy knew that there are night-time *and* daytime ones as well!'

'But,' began George again, and stopped as Mr Gringle gave her quite a glare.

'This is a Six-Spot Burnet Day-Flying moth,' he said speaking slowly as if he were addressing a very small child. 'It loves to fly in the hot sunshine. Please don't argue with me. I don't like ignorance of this sort.'

George looked rather mutinous and Dick nudged her. 'He's right,' he said in a low voice. 'You don't know much about moths, so say nothing, George, or he won't let us go with him.'

'I'd like two or three more of these Six-Spots highly coloured and unusually large. Perhaps you'd see if you can find any more, all of you.'

Everybody began to look here and there, and to shake any little bush or clump of grass they passed. Timmy and Binky were very interested in this and began a hunt on their own, sniffing and snuffling everywhere, not quite sure what they were looking for, but enjoying it all the same.

Mr Gringle took a long time to get to his butterfly farm, and the children began to wish they hadn't asked to go. There was so much side-stepping to see this and that, so much examining when a specimen was caught, so much 'talky-talk', as Dick whispered to Anne.

'Do you keep your butterflies and moths in those glasshouses?' asked Julian.

'Yes,' said Mr Gringle. 'Come along – I'll show you what I and my colleague Mr Brent do. He's away today, so you can't meet him.'

It was certainly a strange place. The cottage

looked as if it were about to fall down at any moment. Two of the windows were broken and some tiles had fallen off the roof. But the glasshouses were in good repair, and the glass panes were perfectly clean. Evidently the butterfly men thought more of their butterflies and moths than they did of themselves.

'Do you live here all alone with Mr Brent, your colleague?' asked Dick curiously, thinking that it must be a strange and lonely life.

'Oh, no. Old Mrs Janes lives here too,' said Mr Gringle. 'And sometimes her son comes to do my small repairs, and to clean all the glass of the butterfly houses. There's the old lady, look. She can't bear insects of any sort, so she never comes into the glasshouses.'

An old woman, looking exactly like a witch, peered out at them through a window in the cottage. Anne was quite scared to see her. Toby grinned.

'She's harmless,' he said to Anne. 'She often comes to us for eggs and milk. She's got no teeth at all, so she mutters and mumbles and that makes her seem more like a witch than ever.'

'I don't much like the look of her,' said Anne,

going thankfully into the first of the butterfly houses. 'Oh – what a lot of butterflies!'

There certainly were! Hundreds were flying about loose, and many others were in little compartments either by themselves or with another butterfly to match.

The children saw that many bushes and plants were growing in the glasshouse, and on some of them were placed long sleeves made of muslin, tied in at each end.

'What's in these long sleeves of fine muslin?' asked Dick. 'Oh – I see. They're full of caterpillars! How they're eating, too!'

'Yes. I told you we breed butterflies and moths,' said Mr Gringle, and he opened the end of one of the muslin bags, so that the visitors could see the caterpillars better. 'These are the caterpillars of one kind of butterfly; they feed on this particular plant.'

The children gazed at dozens of green caterpillars, marked with red and yellow spots, all eating greedily on the leaves of the twig enclosed there. Mr Gringle undid another of the muslin bags and showed them some huge caterpillars, each of them green, with purple stripes on the side and a strange black horn on the tail end.

'Privet-Hawk moth caterpillars,' said Mr Gringle, and Julian and Dick nodded. They knew these big green caterpillars quite well.

'Why is the moth called Privet-*Hawk*?' asked Anne. 'There are so many different Hawk moths, I know. I've often wondered why they're all called *Hawk*.'

Mr Gringle beamed at Anne, evidently thinking that this was an intelligent question.

'Haven't you ever seen a Hawk moth flying?' he said. 'No? Well, it flies very strongly indeed. Oh, a very striking flight – like the flight of the *bird* called a hawk, you know.'

'You're not feeding the caterpillars on privet, though,' said George. 'But you *said* they were Privet-Hawks.'

'There isn't any privet growing near here,' said Mr Gringle. 'So I give them elder – this is an elder bush which I planted in the glasshouse. They like it just as much.'

The butterfly farm was certainly interesting, and the children wandered about the glasshouse watching caterpillars of all kinds, admiring the lovely specimens of butterflies, and marvelling at the collection of strangely shaped chrysalides and cocoons that Mr Gringle kept carefully in boxes, waiting for the perfect insect, moth or butterfly, to emerge.

'Like magic,' he said in an awed voice, his eyes shining behind his glasses. 'Sometimes, you know, I feel like a magician myself – and my butterfly net is a wand!'

The children felt rather uncomfortable as he said this, waving his butterfly net to and fro like a wand. He really was rather an odd person.

'It's very hot in here,' said Julian suddenly. 'Let's get into the fresh air. I've had enough. Goodbye, Mr Gringle, and thank you!'

Out they all went and drew in deep breaths of fresh air. And then they heard a croaking voice behind them.

'Get out of here!' said the voice. 'Get out!'

7 Mrs Janes – a spider – and a pool

Timmy growled, and so did Binky. The children swung round and saw the witch-like woman standing there, her wispy grey hair hanging over her face.

'What's the matter, Mrs – er – Mrs Janes?' said Julian, fortunately remembering the name Mr Gringle had told them. 'We're not doing any harm.'

'My son doesn't like strangers here,' said Mrs Janes, mumbling so much that the children could hardly understand what she was saying.

'But this place belongs to Mr Gringle surely, and his friend,' said Dick, puzzled.

'I tell you my son doesn't like strangers here,' mumbled the woman again and shook her fist at them.

Timmy didn't like this, and growled. She at once pointed her finger at him and muttered a long string of strange-sounding words so that Anne shrank back, afraid. Really, Mrs Janes did look exactly like a witch – and sounded like one, too.

Timmy acted strangely. He put his tail down, stopped growling and crept close to George. She was astonished.

'It looks as if she's trying to put a spell on Tim,' said Dick, half laughing, but that was too much for Anne and George.

Taking Timmy by the collar, George rushed off quickly with Anne following. The boys laughed. Binky ran after Timmy, and Toby spoke boldly to the funny woman.

'Your son isn't even here – so what business is it of his to tell you to give orders to visitors?'

Tears suddenly began to pour down the woman's face and she wrung her bony hands together.

'He'll hit me,' she wept. 'He'll twist my arm! Go away! Please go away! If he comes, he'll chase you off. He's a bad man, my son!'

'She's confused, poor old thing,' said Toby, feeling sorry for Mrs Janes. 'But she's harmless enough. Her son's not too bad – he's quite good at repairs, and we used to have him come to the farm to mend roofs and things like that. But he's not as good as he used to be. Come on – let's go. Mr Gringle's a bit strange, too, isn't he?'

They went off after the two girls, Toby still feeling uncomfortable and distressed.

'What's Mr Gringle's friend like – the one who helps him?' Julian asked.

'I don't know. I've never seen him,' said Toby. 'He's away mostly, doing the business side, I think – selling specimens of eggs, caterpillars and so on – and the perfect moths and butterflies too, of course.'

'I'd like to see that butterfly house again, but Mr Gringle gets on my nerves,' said Dick. 'Those shiny eyes behind those thick glasses. You'd think that if they were as bright and piercing as that he wouldn't need to wear any glasses at all!'

'Hey, George – Anne!' shouted Julian. 'Wait for us – we're just coming.'

They caught up with the girls and Julian grinned at George.

'You thought Timmy was going to be changed into a black beetle or something, didn't you?' he said.

'No, of course not,' said George, going red. 'I just didn't like her very much – pointing her finger like that at Timmy. No wonder he growled.'

'You didn't hear what she said about her son,' said Dick. 'She began to cry like anything after you'd gone, and say that her son would beat her and twist her arm if we didn't go – and he's not even there!'

'She's mad,' said George. 'I don't want to go there again. What are we going to do now?'

'Go up to our camping place and have our lunch,' said Julian promptly. 'Come with us, Toby – or have you got jobs to do at the farm?'

'No. I've done them all,' said Toby. 'I'd love to have a meal with you up on the hill.'

It wasn't very long before they were back at their camping place. Everything was as they had left it – anoraks neatly under the gorse bush with the rugs and other little things – and the food in Anne's 'larder' waiting for them.

The meal was very hilarious, as Toby was in one of his silly moods, and produced some idiotic jokes. The most successful one was a large imitation spider with shaky legs, which, while Anne and George had gone to get the food, he hung by a thin nylon thread to a spray on the nearby gorse bush. Dick grinned broadly.

'Wait till Anne sees that!' he said. 'George always says *she* doesn't mind spiders, but a big one like that's pretty creepy.'

It certainly was. Anne didn't spot it until she was eating her strawberries, covered with some of the cream that Toby's mother had generously sent. Then she suddenly saw it, shaking slightly in the breeze, hanging by its thread just over George's head.

'Oooooooooh!' she squealed. 'Ooooh, George – be careful! There's a MONSTER spider just over your head!'

'What – is George scared of spiders?' cried Toby at once. 'Typical girl!'

George glared at him. 'I don't mind them at all,' she said coldly.

'*George* – please move!' cried Anne, upsetting her strawberries in her anxiety. 'It's almost on your head, I tell you – its legs are wobbling as if they're going to settle on your hair. George, it's an ENORMOUS one! It might even be one of those dangerous things – a tarantula or something!'

The wind blew a little just then and the spider

moved about on the thread very realistically. Even Dick was glad it wasn't alive!

George couldn't resist looking up, pretending to be quite calm – but when she saw the enormous creature just above her she shot straight out of her place and landed on Toby's legs, making him spill his strawberries and cream.

'Now, now, Georgina,' said the annoying Toby, picking up his strawberries. 'You said you didn't *mind* spiders. I'll remove it for you, and you can go back to your place.'

'No, no – don't touch it – ugh!' cried Anne. But Toby, putting on a very brave face, leaned over and neatly took the spider off the gorse bush, still swinging by its thread. He swung it near to Anne, who scrambled up at once.

Then he made it 'walk' over Dick's knee, and Timmy came to investigate at once. Binky came too, and snapped at it, breaking the nylon thread that held it.

'Idiot!' said Toby, giving him a smack. 'My beautiful spider – my spinner of webs – my tame catcher of flies!'

'What – is it a *tame* one?' said Anne in horror.

'More or less,' said Toby, and put it carefully

into his pocket, grinning all over his round face.

'That's enough, Toby,' said Julian. 'Joke's over.'

George stared at Toby, her face growing crimson. 'A joke? A JOKE! You wait till I pay you back, Toby! I don't call that a joke . . . I call it a mean trick. You knew Anne hated spiders.'

'Let's change the subject,' said Dick hastily. 'What are we going to do this afternoon?'

'I know what I'd *like* to do,' said Julian longingly. 'I'd like a swim. It's so hot. If we were at Kirrin I'd be in the sea all the afternoon.'

'I wish we *were* at Kirrin,' said George sulkily.

'Well – if you really do want a swim, I can take you to a pool,' said Toby, anxious to get into everyone's good books again.

'A pool? Where?' said Dick eagerly.

'Well – see that airfield down there?' said Toby pointing. 'And see this spring here, where you get your water? It goes on and on running down the hill, joins two or three more little rivulets, and ends in a fantastic pool not far from the airfield. Cold as ice it is, too. I've often swum there.'

'It sounds really good,' said Julian, pleased. 'Well, we can't swim immediately after a meal.

We'll do the washing up, and put the rest of the food away. Then we'll sit here and have a bit of a rest, and then go and find this pool.'

Everyone agreed to this and they all set to work.

'If Toby has any more idiotic tricks like that I'll play a few on *him*!' said George. 'In fact I've a good mind to pull him under in the pool.'

'He's all right, George,' said Anne. 'He's just like that at school, Dick says. He must drive the teachers mad!'

They all had a short rest, while Timmy and Binky went off amiably together to do a little hunting – sniffing down holes and under bushes, looking very serious indeed. They came back immediately George whistled.

'We're going, Timmy,' said George. 'Here are your swimming things, Dick, and yours, Julian. Good thing we brought them with us!'

'What about you, Toby? You haven't got anything with you,' said Julian.

'We have to pass fairly near the farm,' said Toby. 'I'll leave you when we're near there and get mine – it won't take more than five minutes if I run all the way back.'

They set off down the hill towards the airfield. Except for the plane they had heard that morning, they had heard and seen none. It seemed a very quiet airfield.

'Wait till they start experimenting with the new fighter planes my cousin told me about!' said Toby. 'You'll hear a noise then – they're so fast they break the sound barrier every time they go up!'

'Would your cousin let us look around the airfield one day?' asked Julian. 'I'd like to do that. Look – isn't that your farm, Toby? We've got here really quickly – but it's all downhill, of course.'

'Yes,' said Toby. 'Come on, Binky – race you home and back. Won't be long, Julian! Keep straight ahead and walk towards that big pine tree you can see in the distance. I'll be with you by the time you're there.'

He raced off at top speed, while the others went on slowly towards the pine trees in the distance. It would be lovely to swim in a cool pool!

Toby was certainly a fast runner! Just before they reached the pine tree he came up behind them, his swimming things over his shoulder, so out of breath that he could hardly speak!

'It's over there,' he panted. 'Look – the pool!'

And sure enough, there was the pool – deep blue, cool and as smooth as glass. Trees surrounded it on one side, and heather grew right down to the edge.

The five children went towards it gladly – but suddenly they came to a big notice, nailed to a tree:

KEEP OUT

DANGER

CROWN PROPERTY

'What does *that* mean?' said Dick in dismay. 'We can't swim after all!'

'Oh, take no notice of that,' said Toby. 'It doesn't mean a thing!'

But it did, as they were very soon to find out!

8 *A spot of trouble*

'Why do you say that the notice doesn't mean a thing?' said Julian. 'Why put it up, then?'

'Oh, there are notices like that all round the airfield,' said Toby airily. 'Telling you to KEEP OUT, there's DANGER. But there isn't. Only aeroplanes are here, no guns, no bombs, nothing. It's a really lonely place, too, tucked away at the foot of this hill.'

'Why don't you ask your cousin *why* they put up the notices?' asked Dick. 'There must be some reason!'

'I tell you those notices have been up for ages,' said Toby, sounding cross. 'Ages! They might have been some use at some time or other, but not now. We can swim here and do what we like.'

'All right – but I hope you know what you're talking about,' said Julian. 'I suppose I can't see any sense in putting notices here – there's no wire or fencing to keep anyone out.'

'Let's get into our swimming things, then,' said Dick. 'You girls can have that bush over there and we'll have this one. Hurry up!'

They were soon changed into their swimsuits, and dived into the pool, which was surprisingly deep. It was also deliciously cool, and silky to the touch, just as the spring water had been. The two dogs leapt in gladly and swam vigorously round and round. The children splashed them, and Timmy began to bark excitedly.

'Quiet, Timmy!' said Toby at once.

'Why should he?' demanded George, swimming up.

'Well – someone at the airfield might hear him,' said Toby.

'You said it didn't matter us being here!' said George. 'Look out for yourself!'

She dived underwater and got hold of Toby's legs, pulling him down. He yelled and kicked and spluttered, but George was strong and she gave him a very, very good ducking! He came up purple in the face.

'I said I'd pay you back for the spider!' yelled George, and swam strongly away.

Toby swam after her, and she led him a fine

dance round the pool, for she was a very good swimmer. The others laughed at the contest.

'I back George,' said Dick. 'She'd outswim most boys. Well, she's put Toby in his place all right. He won't be so free with spiders and silly jokes for a while!'

Timmy began to bark again when he saw Toby chasing George, and Binky joined in.

'Quiet, Binky!' shouted Toby. 'I tell you *stop barking*!'

Before Binky had obeyed, something happened. A very loud voice came across the pool.

'What's all this! You're trespassing on Crown property. Didn't you see the notice?'

The dogs stopped barking and the five children looked round to see who was shouting. Their heads bobbed on the surface of the water as they gazed about to find the shouter.

It was a man in Air Force uniform, a big man, burly and red-faced.

'What's the matter?' called Julian, swimming towards him. 'We're only swimming. We're not doing any harm.'

'Didn't you see the notice?' shouted the man, pointing over to it.

'Yes. But we couldn't see much danger here,' called back Julian, wishing now that he hadn't believed Toby.

'You come on out!' roared the man. 'All of you. Come on.'

They all waded out of the cool pond, Anne feeling scared. The dogs splashed out, too, and stood eyeing the man grimly. He calmed down a little when he saw them.

'Those your dogs I heard barking? Well, now, I see you're all kids – although one of you's big enough to know better!' and he pointed to Julian. 'I thought maybe you were tourists – thinking you could come wandering on the airfield and not get into trouble!'

'Tourists don't come here,' said Toby, squeezing the water out of his hair.

'Nor do sensible children,' retorted the man. 'I've had trouble from you before, haven't I? Yes. Didn't you come walking round the hangars one day? And that dog with you, too?'

'I only went to see my cousin, Flight-Lieutenant Thomas,' said Toby. 'I wasn't doing any harm – I wasn't spying. I only went to see my cousin!'

'Well, I'll report you to him,' said the man, 'and

tell him to give you a proper telling off. We've got strict instructions to warn off anyone – there's notices everywhere.'

'Is something hush-hush going on then?' said Toby with a sudden grin.

'As if I'd tell you if there was!' said the man in disgust. 'Far as I can see, there's nothing much going on here – dull as ditchwater this place – and as far as I'm concerned I'd welcome a *horde* of tourists – it would liven up the place no end. But orders are orders, as you very well know.'

Julian thought it was about time that he should join in. The man was only doing his duty, and Toby was silly to have said that the notices meant nothing.

'Well, we apologise for trespassing,' he said in his clear, pleasant voice. 'We won't swim here again, I promise you. Sorry to have made you come all this way to warn us off.'

The RAF guard looked at Julian with respect. There was something about the boy that reassured people, and the man now felt sure that it was all Toby's fault. He smiled.

'That's all right,' he said. 'Sorry to cut your swim short this hot day. And – er – if that rogue of a boy here' – he pointed to Toby – 'if he cares to ask Flight-Lieutenant Thomas for permission to swim in this pool at certain hours, it's OK by me. I won't come running then when I hear dogs barking and a lot of shouting if I know you're allowed here at certain hours.'

'Thanks,' said Julian. 'But anyway we're only here for a few days.'

'Goodbye,' said the man and walked off briskly.

'Well,' said Toby, completely unashamed, 'what did he want to come messing about here for, spoiling our swim? He *said* there wasn't anything secret going on, so why—'

'Oh be quiet!' said Dick. 'You heard what he said about orders being orders? He's not a silly schoolkid trying to be clever and getting out of doing his work – yes, like *you* do at school, Toby, and plenty of the others! He's a man in uniform. Grow up a bit.'

'I agree,' said Julian. 'So don't let's hear any more about it. You made a mistake, Toby, and that's all there is to it. Now let's dry ourselves and go to the farm and ask your nice kind mum if she'll let us have some more food to take back to

our camp with us. I'm as hungry as a hunter after
our swim.'

Toby was rather subdued after all this. He
glanced at George to see if she was smirking over
his telling off, but George was never one to gloat
over anyone's downfall, and Toby felt relieved.

'*Shall* I ask my cousin if he'll get permission for
us to swim in the pool?' he said as they went away
from the water, dry and dressed again.

'I think not,' said Julian. 'But I'd like to meet
your cousin some time all the same.'

'He *might* take us up in a plane,' said Toby
hopefully, his spirits rising at the thought. 'Oh,
look there – here's that little pain Benny again –
and the piglet!'

Benny panted up, carrying the little pig. 'You
look like Tom, Tom the Piper's Son,' said Julian,
ruffling the yellow curls. 'He stole a pig and ran
away, carrying it under his arm.'

'But this is my own pig,' said Benny, surprised.
'I didn't steal him. I came to find you, because my
mum says come to tea.'

'You *have* got a nice mum!' said Anne, taking
the small boy's hand. 'Why don't you put the pig
down? He must be so heavy.'

'He runned away again,' said Benny severely. 'So I carried him.'

'Put a collar on his neck, with a lead,' suggested Dick.

'He hasn't got a neck,' said Benny, and indeed the piglet was so plump that his head joined his body without any neck at all.

The little procession made its way to the farm, and the piglet at once ran in front, squealing. It seemed surprised and delighted to find it was home again. Timmy pricked up his ears when it squealed. He thought that it must be in pain, and he was worried! He ran beside the little creature, trying to nuzzle it.

Mrs Thomas saw them through the window. 'Come along in!' she said. 'I thought you might like to have tea here again today, because I've a visitor you'd like to meet!'

'Who is it?' cried Toby, running indoors. 'Oh! it's you, Cousin Jeff. Hey, Julian, Dick – look, it's my Cousin Jeff from the airfield – Flight-Lieutenant Thomas! The one I told you about! Cousin Jeff, meet my friends – Julian, Dick, Anne, Georgina – er, I mean George – and Timmy!'

A tall, good-looking young man stood up,

smiling. The Five gazed at him, liking him very much indeed. They all envied Toby at that moment. No wonder he'd boasted about him so much!

'Hello to you!' said Cousin Jeff. 'Glad to see you all. Hey – look at this dog!'

And well might everyone look, for Timmy had marched straight up to him and then held up a paw. 'Wuff!' he said, which, of course, meant 'Shake'!

'How do you do?' said Cousin Jeff solemnly, and shook paws with Timmy at once.

'Timmy's *never* done that before!' said George, astonished. 'Well – what a surprising thing! He must like you *very* much!'

9 *Cousin Jeff*

'I like dogs,' said Jeff, and patted Timmy on the head. 'This is a lovely one – clever too, isn't he?'

George nodded, pleased. She loved anyone to praise Timmy. 'Yes, he's very clever. He's been in lots of adventures with us. He can be very fierce if he thinks anyone's going to attack us. Oh, look – he wants to shake hands *again*! Isn't he funny!'

Jeff shook paws once more and then Timmy settled down beside him, almost as if he considered himself to be his dog. George didn't mind. She liked Cousin Jeff as much as Timmy did!

'Tell us about your job,' begged Dick. 'It's such a strange airfield, the one you're at – no fencing round it, hardly any planes, nobody around the field! Do you do much flying?'

'Not much at the moment,' said Cousin Jeff. 'But don't be misled by the fact that there's no fencing round the airfield! Believe me, the commanding officer knows immediately if any stranger comes into the district, and – er – well, let us say that extra precautions are taken.'

'*Really*?' said George. 'Do you mean to say, for instance, that your commanding officer knows *we've* arrived?'

'You bet he does,' said Jeff, laughing. 'You've probably been given the once-over already, although you didn't know it. I expect someone has been detailed to find out who you are and why you're here, and you may even have been watched for a few hours – although you had no idea of it.'

This was rather a creepy thought. Watched? How? By whom? And where did they hide to watch? Dick asked Jeff these questions, but the young airman shook his head.

'Sorry. Can't answer,' he said. 'But you needn't worry, *you're* all right. Maybe my aunt here has said a few words about you – you never know!'

Mrs Thomas smiled, but said nothing. She bustled about, setting out cups and saucers, while the children talked to Cousin Jeff and asked him eager questions about planes and flying and how this was done and that.

'I suppose you wouldn't take us up some time,

Cousin Jeff, would you?' asked Toby at last.

'I don't think I'd be allowed to,' said Jeff. 'In fact I don't think I can even ask. You see, the planes there are pretty special – you can't go joy-riding in them and—'

'Of course we see,' said Julian hurriedly, afraid of embarrassing the friendly young airman. 'We wouldn't *dream* of bothering you. When are you going up next? Can we watch you from our camping place?'

'Yes, I expect you could see me with binoculars,' said Jeff, considering. 'I'll tell you the number of my plane – it's painted underneath it, of course, so you'll know it's me if you see it circling over the hill. But I won't do any stunts, I'm afraid – like coming down low to you, or anything like that. Only silly beginners do that.'

'We'll look out for you,' said Dick, quite envious of Toby for having such an exciting young cousin. 'I don't expect you'll see us – but we'll wave anyway!'

Tea was now ready and they all drew up their chairs. Benny wandered in with his piglet under his arm, and set it down in the cat's basket, where it stayed peacefully, falling asleep and making tiny, grunting snores.

'Does the cat mind?' asked George, astonished, looking at the basket.

'Not a bit,' said Mrs Thomas. 'It had to put up with two goslings last year in its basket – and something the year before . . .'

'A lamb,' said Toby.

'Oh yes – and old Tinky – that's the cat – didn't seem to worry at all,' said Mrs Thomas, pouring out creamy milk for everyone, even Cousin Jeff. 'I once found her curled up round the goslings one morning, purring loudly.'

'Good old Tinky!' said Toby. 'Where is she? I'd like to see what she thinks of Curly. She couldn't cuddle *him* – he takes up nearly all the basket, he's so plump.'

Tea was a happy meal, with Toby playing the fool, putting a spoonful of sifted sugar on the side of Anne's plate to eat with her crisp radishes instead of salt, and offering the salt to George to eat with her strawberries.

Both girls were listening so intently to Cousin Jeff that they didn't even notice what Toby had done, and he almost fell off his chair with laughing when he saw their faces. Salt with strawberries –

ugh! Sugar and radishes – ugh!'

'Funny boy, aren't you?' said George, annoyed at being tricked. 'You wait!' But Toby was too wily to be tricked and George had to give it up. Anyway, she couldn't bother with Toby when Cousin Jeff was talking about planes, his eyes shining with pleasure. Flying was his great love, and in listening to him all three boys there made up their minds to take it up as soon as they could!

Benny didn't listen much. He was more interested in animals than in planes. He ate his tea solemnly and watched his piglet in the cat's basket, occasionally leaning over to tap his mother's hand when he wanted to speak to her.

'Curly runned away again,' he told her solemnly. 'Right up to the horse-pond.'

'I thought I told you not to go there,' said his mother. 'You fell in last time.'

'But Curly *runned* there,' said Benny, his big eyes looking very wide and innocent. 'I had to go after him, didn't I? He's my piglet.'

'Well, I'll tell Curly off if he takes you to places you've been told not to go to,' said his mother. 'I can't let him grow up disobedient, can I?'

This needed thinking over, and Benny ate his tea with a serious face, ignoring the others. Anne looked at him several times, delighted with the solemn little boy and his funny ways. How nice it would be to have a small brother like that!

'Well, I must be off,' said Jeff when the meal was finished. 'Thanks for a delicious tea, Aunt Sarah – but then your teas always *are* delicious! I was very lucky to be stationed here so near to Billycock Farm! Well, bye, everyone! Bye, Timmy!'

Everyone went with him to the gate, Timmy and Binky as well, and Benny awoke his little pig and carried him to the gate too, squealing and kicking. They all watched the tall, sturdy young airman striding away round the hill.

'Do you like him?' asked Toby proudly. 'Isn't he wonderful? I'm so proud of him. He's supposed to be one of the cleverest flying men in the country – did you know?'

'No, we didn't,' said Dick. 'But I'm not surprised. He's got eyes as keen as a hawk's, and his heart and soul are in his work! How lucky for you that he's stationed so near!'

'We'd better get back to our camp when we've

helped your mum to clear away and wash up,' said Julian, anxious not to outstay his welcome at the farm. 'Toby, can you pack us up a bit more food in case we don't see you tomorrow?'

'Right,' said Toby, and went off, whistling.

Benny appeared again with Curly running round his feet.

'Hello!' said Dick with a grin. 'Is that piglet of yours running away again?'

Benny grinned back. 'If he runned away to your camp, would you be cross?' he asked, looking very innocently up at Dick.

'He mustn't do that,' said Dick seriously, guessing what was in the little boy's mind; he meant to go to find the camp himself, and then say that it was Curly who had 'runned away' there! 'You see, you might lose your way if you went so far.'

Benny said no more, but wandered off with his comical pet running in front of him. The boys went to find Toby to see if they could help him to pack food into a basket. 'We must pay his bill, too,' said Julian, feeling for his purse. 'It was a good idea of his to save up the money to buy his mum a present. She's really nice.'

Soon the Five were on their way back to their camp again. Toby was left behind to do his usual jobs of collecting the eggs, washing them and grading them into sizes for the market.

'I'll be up tomorrow!' he called after them. 'We'll plan something good to do – maybe visit the caves if you like!'

The four children went up the steep slope of Billycock Hill, talking, while Timmy ranged in front, sniffing everywhere as usual. And then suddenly a large butterfly sailed through the air, and came to rest on a flower of a blossoming elder bush, just in front of George – a butterfly that none of them had ever seen before.

'Look at that! What is it?' cried Anne in delight. 'Oh, it's beautiful! Julian, what is it?'

'I've absolutely no idea!' said Julian, astonished. 'It may be an unusual Fritillary, although it's early in the year for those. That butterfly man – what's his name now? – Mr Gringle – said that this hill was famous for rare butterflies, and I imagine this is pretty uncommon. It *is* beautiful, isn't it?'

They watched the butterfly opening and shutting its magnificent wings on the white blossom.

'We ought to try and catch it,' said Dick. 'I bet Mr Gringle would be thrilled. It might lay eggs for him and start a whole breed of rare butterflies in this country.'

'I've got a very thin hanky,' said Anne. 'I think I can catch it without harming its wings – and we'll put it into the little box that Toby filled with sugar lumps for us. Get it and empty it, Dick.'

In half a minute the butterfly was inside the box, completely unharmed, for Anne had been very deft in catching it.

'What a wonderful creature!' said Dick, shutting the box. 'Now come on – we'll give Mr Gringle a surprise!'

'What about that witch woman – you know, Mrs Janes, who looks exactly like a witch?' said Anne. 'I don't want to meet her again.'

'I'll tell her to jump on her broomstick and fly away!' said Julian with a laugh. 'Don't be silly, Anne – she can't hurt you.'

They went off round the hill, taking the little path down which Mr Gringle had guided them. Soon they saw the reflection of the sun glittering on the glasshouses. Anne and George hesitated as they came near, and Timmy stopped, too, his tail down.

'Well, stay there, then,' said Dick impatiently. 'Ju and I won't be long!'

And off went the two boys together, while George and Anne waited in the distance.

'I hope they *won't* be long!' said Anne, worried. 'I don't know *why* I feel creepy here, but I do!'

10 *Butterfly farm again*

Dick and Julian went to the glasshouses where the butterflies and caterpillars lived. They peered through the panes, but could see nobody there.

'Mr Gringle must be in the cottage,' said Julian. 'Let's stand outside and call – he'll come out then. I don't much like Mrs Janes.'

So they stood outside the tumbledown cottage and shouted: 'Mr Gringle! Mr Gringle!'

Nobody answered. No Mr Gringle came out, but somebody pulled aside the corner of a window curtain upstairs and peered out. The boys shouted again, waving at the window.

'Mr Gringle! We've got a rare butterfly for you!'

The window opened and old Mrs Janes looked out, seeming more witch-like than ever.

'Mr Gringle's away!' she mumbled.

'What about his colleague Mr Brent – the one we didn't see?' shouted Dick. 'Is he in?'

The old woman stared at them, mumbled something else, and then disappeared very suddenly indeed from the window.

Dick looked at Julian in surprise.

'Why did she go so suddenly? Almost as if somebody pulled her roughly away? Julian, I don't like it.'

'Why? Do you think that son of hers is here – the one she said was cruel to her?' asked Julian, who was puzzled, too.

'I don't know,' said Dick. 'Let's snoop around a bit. Perhaps Mr Gringle *is* somewhere about, whatever old Mrs Janes says!'

They went round the corner of the house and peered into a shed. Nobody there. Then they heard footsteps and turned round hurriedly. A man was coming towards them, small and thin, with a pinched-looking face, and dark glasses. He carried a butterfly net, and nodded at the two boys.

'My colleague Gringle is away,' he said. 'Can I do anything for you?'

'Oh – you're Mr Brent then?' said Dick. 'Look – we've found a rare butterfly. That's why we came!'

He undid the box in which the butterfly was peacefully resting, having found a tiny grain of sugar to feed on. Mr Brent looked at it through his dark glasses.

'Hmm! Hmm!' he said, peering closely at it. 'Yes, very good indeed. I'll buy it off you.'

'Oh, you can have it for nothing,' said Dick. 'What is it?'

'Can't say without examining it closely,' said Mr Brent, and took the box and put the lid on again.

'But isn't it some kind of Fritillary?' asked Julian. 'We thought it was.'

'Quite likely,' said Mr Brent, and suddenly produced a coin and shoved it at Dick. 'Here you are. Much obliged. I'll tell Mr Gringle you came.'

He turned abruptly and went off, his butterfly net still over his shoulder.

Dick stared at the coin in his hand, then at the receding back of Mr Brent.

'What a strange man!' he said. 'Well, he and Mr Gringle are quite a pair! What should we do with this money, Julian? I don't want it!'

'Let's see if we can give it to that poor Mrs

Janes,' said Julian, always generous. 'She looks as if they paid her nothing, poor thing.'

They went round to the front of the house, hoping to find the old woman, and after a little hesitation knocked at the door. It opened and she stood there, mumbling as before.

'You go away! My son's coming back. He'll hit me. He doesn't like strangers. You go away, I say!'

'All right,' said Dick. 'Look – here's something for you,' and he pressed the coin into her claw-like hand.

She looked at it as if she couldn't believe her eyes, and then, amazingly quickly she slipped the money into one of her broken-down shoes. When she stood up her eyes were full of tears.

'You're kind,' she whispered, and gave them a little push. 'Yes, you're kind. Keep away from here. My son's a bad man. Keep away!'

The boys went off silently, not knowing what to make of it. After all, Toby knew the son – they had employed him at the farm. Why did the woman keep saying he was bad and cruel? She must be very confused to talk like that!

'It must be a strange household,' said Julian

as they went to join the waiting girls. 'Two butterfly men, both rather odd. One witch-like woman, very odd. And a son who seems to terrify her out of her wits! I vote we don't go there again.'

'So do I,' said Dick. 'Hello, you two – did we keep you waiting for long?'

'Yes, you did,' said Anne. 'We were just about to send Timmy to look for you! We thought you might have been turned into mice, or something!'

The boys told the two girls about Mr Brent and the money and old Mrs Janes. 'A funny household,' said Dick. 'We think we'll give it a miss now, however many rare butterflies we spot! I'm pretty certain that the one we found was a kind of Fritillary, aren't you, Julian?'

'Yes, I was surprised Mr Brent didn't say so,' said Julian. 'I have a feeling that Mr Gringle is the expert of the two. Mr Brent probably does the donkey-work – sees to the caterpillars and so on.'

They came to their camp at last, and Timmy at once went to the 'larder'. But Anne shook her head. 'No, Tim – it's not nearly supper-time. Bad luck!'

'What shall we do?' asked Dick, flinging himself down on the heather. 'It's another gorgeous evening!'

'Yes – but I don't much like the look of the sky over to the west tonight,' said Julian. 'See those clouds there coming up slowly against the wind? It looks like rain tomorrow to me!'

'Oh no!' said George. 'The weather might have lasted for just one week! What'll we do if it pours? Sit in our tents all day, I suppose!'

'Cheer up – we could go and see the caves,' said Dick. 'I know what we'll do now! We'll get out our portable radio and turn it on. If there's some decent music, it'll sound amazing up here!'

'All right. But please let's have it on softly,' said Anne. 'I can't *stand* people who take radios out into the country with them, and switch them on loudly, so that it spoils the peace and quiet for everyone else. I could go and kick their radios to pieces!'

'Anne – you do sound fierce!' said George, looking at her cousin in surprise.

'You don't know our quiet sister Anne quite as well as we do, George,' said Julian, with a twinkle in his eyes. 'She can be really fierce if she thinks anyone's spoiling things for others. I had to stop her once from going up to tell people off at a picnic – they actually had their music going full-blast, in spite of the angry looks from people all around. I honestly think she meant to turn off the stereo and break it over somebody's head!'

'Oh, *Julian*! How can you say that!' said Anne. 'I did feel like it – but I didn't do it.'

'All right, Anne!' said Julian affectionately and patted her head.

Both he and Dick thought the world of their quiet, kind little sister. She smiled at them.

'Well – let's have some music, then,' she said. 'There's the Pastoral Symphony on sometime this evening, I know, because I made a note of it. It'd sound beautiful out here in this lovely countryside with that view spreading for miles in front of us. But softly, *please*.'

Julian fetched the little radio and took it out of its waterproof case. He switched on, and a voice came loudly from it. Julian lowered the volume to make it softer. 'It's the seven o'clock news,' he said. 'We'll hear it, shall we?'

But it was almost the end of the news, and the voice soon stopped to give way to an announcer.

Yes – it was going to be the Pastoral Symphony now. Soon the first notes came softly from the little radio, and it seemed to set the countryside around to music. The four settled down in the heather to listen, lying half propped up to watch the changing colours of the view in front of them as the sun sank lower.

The bank of cloud on the horizon was higher now, and the sun would soon slip behind it, for it was coming up fast. What a pity!

And then, cutting across the music, came another sound – the sound of an aeroplane.

R-r-r-r-r-r-r! R-r-r-r-r-r! R-r-r-r-r-r!

It sounded so very loud that Dick and Julian leapt to their feet, and Timmy began to bark loudly.

'Where is it?' said Dick, puzzled. 'It sounds so near. I wonder if it's Cousin Jeff's!'

'There it is – coming up over the back of the hill!' said Julian, and as he spoke a small aeroplane appeared over the brow of the hill, and circled once before it flew down to the airfield.

The four children could clearly see the number painted underneath. '5–6–9,' began Julian, and Dick gave a shout.

'It's Jeff's plane! It is – that's his number! Wave, everybody, wave!'

So they all waved madly, although they felt sure that Jeff wouldn't see them, tucked away in their camp on the hillside. They watched the plane fly down to the airfield, circle round, and land neatly on the runway. It came to a stop.

Julian looked through his binoculars and saw a small figure leap from the plane. 'I bet it's Jeff,' he said. 'Oh – I wish *I* had a plane to fly over the hills and far away!'

11 *A stormy night*

The Five soon began to prepare for their evening meal and Timmy trotted about pretending to help, always hopeful of being allowed to carry a loaf of bread or piece of cold ham in his mouth. But he was never lucky!

As they sat eating their meal, Julian glanced uneasily at the western sky again. 'The rain's certainly coming,' he said. 'That cloud has covered half the sky now, and swallowed up the evening sun. I think we should put up the tents.'

'Oh no! I suppose we should,' said George.

'*And* we'd better do it quickly,' said Dick. 'I felt a nasty cold wind just then – the first really cold air since we came here. We'll certainly want to roll up in our rugs tonight!'

'Well, let's get the things out from under the old gorse bush,' said Julian. 'It won't take long to put up the tents if we all get to work.'

In three-quarters of an hour the tents were up,

set nicely in the shelter of the giant gorse bush.

'Good!' said Dick, pleased. 'It'd take a hurricane to blow the tents away – we'll be all right here. Let's pull up some more heather and pile it in the tents. We'll want our rugs to wrap ourselves in, not to lie on tonight, so we might as well make our beds as soft as possible.'

They piled heather into the tents, spread their jackets there, too, and then looked at the sky. Yes, there was no doubt about it – there was rain coming and probably a storm! Still, it might clear tomorrow, and be as sunny as ever. If it wasn't they would go and explore the caves that Toby had told them about.

It was now almost dark and the children decided that they would all get into one tent and have the radio on again. They called Timmy, but he preferred to be outside.

They set the radio going – but almost immediately Timmy began to bark. George switched off at once.

'That's the bark he gives when somebody's coming,' she said. 'I wonder who it is?'

'Toby, to say we'd better go to the farm for the night,' guessed Dick.

'Mr Gringle hunting for moths!' said Anne with a giggle.

'Old Mrs Janes looking for things to make spells with!' said George.

Everyone laughed.

'Very funny!' said Dick. 'Although this looks like a night for witches!'

Timmy went on barking, and Julian put his head out of the tent.

'What's up, Tim?' he said. 'Who's coming?'

'Wuff, wuff,' said Timmy, not turning his head to Julian, but seeming to watch something or someone in the half light.

'It may be a hedgehog he's seen,' said George from inside the tent. 'He always barks at them because he knows he can't pick them up.'

'Well – maybe you're right,' said Julian. 'But I think I'll just go out and get Timmy to take me to whatever it is he's barking at. I'd like to know. He obviously hears or sees something!'

He slid out of the tent opening and went to Timmy.

'Come on, Tim,' he said. 'Who is it? What's upsetting you?'

Timmy wagged his tail and ran in front of

Julian. He obviously had no doubts about where he was going. Julian followed him, stumbling over the heather and wishing he'd brought his torch, for it was now half dark.

Timmy ran some way down the hill towards the airfield, then rounded a clump of birch trees and stopped. He barked loudly again. Julian saw a dark shadow moving there and called out.

'Who's there? Who is it?'

'It's only me – Mr Brent,' said an annoyed voice, and Julian caught sight of a long stick with a shadowy net on the end. 'I've come out to examine our honey-traps before the rain comes and washes away the moths feeding there.'

'Oh,' said Julian. 'I should have thought of that when Timmy barked. Is Mr Gringle about, too?'

'Yes – so if your dog barks again you'll know it's only us,' said Mr Brent. 'We're often prowling around at night – this is just as good a hill for moths at night as it is for butterflies by day. Can't you stop that dog barking at me? Really, he's very badly trained.'

'Quiet, Tim,' ordered Julian, and Timmy obediently closed his mouth, but still stood stiffly, staring at the man in the darkness.

'I'm going on to our next honey-trap,' said the man. 'So you can take that noisy dog back to wherever you're camping.' Mr Brent began to move away, flashing a torch in front of him.

'We're just up the hill,' said Julian. 'About half a kilometre. Oh – you've got a torch, I see. I wish I'd brought mine.'

The man said nothing more, but went slowly on his way, the beam of his torch growing fainter. Julian began to climb back up the hill to the tents, but in the growing darkness it wasn't easy! He missed his way and went much too far to the right. Timmy was puzzled and went to him, tugging gently at his sleeve.

'Am I going wrong?' said Julian. 'I'd soon get lost on this lonely hillside. Dick! George! Anne! Give a shout, will you? I don't know where I am.'

But he had wandered so far off the path that the three didn't hear him – and Timmy had to guide him for a good way before he saw the torches of the others flashing up above. He felt very relieved. He had no wish to be caught in a heavy rainstorm on the exposed side of Billycock Hill!

'Is that you, Julian?' called Anne's anxious voice. 'You've been ages! Did you get lost?'

'Almost!' said Julian. 'Stupidly, I went without my torch – but Timmy here knew the way all right. I'm glad I'm back – it's just beginning to rain!'

'Who was Tim barking at?' asked George.

'One of the butterfly men – Mr Brent, the one Dick and I saw today,' said Julian. 'I just caught the glint of his dark glasses in the half light, and saw the butterfly net he carried. He said Mr Gringle was out, too.'

'But what for, with a storm coming?' asked Anne. 'All the moths would be well in hiding.'

'They've come out to examine their moth-traps, as they call them,' said Julian. 'They spread sticky stuff like honey or something round the trunks of trees – and the moths fly down to it. Then they come along and collect any they want to take back.'

'I see – and I suppose Mr Brent was afraid the rain might wash away the clinging moths,' said Dick. 'Well, they'll both be caught in the storm, that's for sure. Listen to the rain pelting down on the tent now!'

Timmy squeezed into the tent, not liking the sting of the heavy raindrops. He sat down by George and Anne.

'You do take up a lot of room in a small tent, Tim,' said George. 'Can't you make yourself a bit smaller?'

Timmy couldn't. He was a big dog, and rather a sprawly one. He put his wet head on George's knee and heaved a heavy sigh. George patted him.

'Humbug!' she said. 'What are you sighing about? Because you've finished your bone? Because it's raining and you can't go and sit and bark at anything moving on the hill?'

'What shall we do now?' said Julian, setting his torch on the radio, so that it more or less lit up the tent. 'There's nothing on the radio we want to hear.'

'I've got a pack of cards somewhere,' said George, much to everybody's joy, and she found them and got them out. 'Let's have a game of something.'

It was rather difficult in the small tent, with Timmy sometimes getting up just when all the cards were neatly dealt, and upsetting the piles.

The storm grew fiercer and the rain tried its best to lash its way through the canvas of the little tent.

Then Timmy began to bark again, startling everyone very much. He climbed over legs and knees and poked his head out of the tent opening, barking loudly.

'You almost gave me a heart attack!' said Dick, pulling him back. 'You'll get soaked out there, Tim. Come back – it's only those mad moth-men out there picking moths off rain-soaked honey-traps. Don't worry about *them*. They're probably enjoying themselves.'

But Timmy would NOT stop barking, and even growled when Julian tried to drag him into the tent.

'Whatever's up with him?' said Julian, bewildered. 'Oh, stop it, Timmy! You're deafening us!'

'Something's upsetting him – something unusual,' said George. 'Listen – was that a yell?'

Everyone listened, but the rain was pelting down so hard that it was impossible to hear anything but the slashing rain and the wind.

'Well, we can't do much about it, whatever it is

that's upsetting Timmy,' said Dick. 'We can't go wandering about in this storm – we'd get soaked through and probably lost!'

Timmy was still barking, and George grew cross. 'Timmy! Stop! Do you hear me? I won't have it.'

It was so seldom that George was angry with him that Timmy turned in surprise. George pounced at his collar and dragged him forcibly into the tent. 'Now – be QUIET!' she commanded. 'Whatever it is, we can't do anything about it!'

Just then another noise rose above the howling of the wind and the torrents of rain, and the Five pricked up their ears at once, sitting absolutely still.

'R-r-r-r-r-r-r-r-r! R-r-r-r-r-r-r-r-r-r! R-R-R-R-R-R-R-R-R-R-R! R-R-R-R-R-R-R-R-R-R-R!'

They all looked round at one another.

'Aeroplanes!' said Dick. 'Aeroplanes! In this weather, too. What is going on?'

12 What happened in Billycock Caves

The little company in the tent were amazed. Why should aeroplanes take off from the airfield in the middle of a stormy night?

'For experiments in storms, perhaps?' said Dick.

'Perhaps they were aeroplanes *landing* there, not leaving,' suggested Anne.

'Possibly – perhaps seeking the shelter of the airfield when they were caught in this storm,' said Dick. But Julian shook his head.

'No,' he said. 'This airfield is too far off the ordinary air-routes – nobody would bother about it; it's so small for one thing – more a little experimental station than anything else. Any aeroplane in difficulties could easily go to a bigger airfield for shelter or help.'

'I wonder if Jeff went up in one of the two we heard,' said George.

Anne yawned. 'What about going to bed?' she

said. 'This tent is so hot and stuffy that I feel half asleep.'

'Yes – it's getting late,' said Julian, looking at his watch. 'You two girls and Timmy can have this tent – it'll save you going out into the rain. Fasten the flap after we've gone – and yell if you want anything.'

'Right. Goodnight, Ju, goodnight, Dick,' said the girls, and the boys scrambled out into the rain. Anne fastened the flap of the tent, and wrapped her rug round her. She burrowed into her heathery bed and made herself comfortable. George did the same.

'Goodnight,' said Anne, sleepily. 'Keep Tim on your side. I can't bear him on my legs, he's so heavy.'

The Five slept soundly and awoke the next morning to a dismal scene of rain and dark clouds.

'*How* disappointing!' said Dick, peering out of his tent. 'We ought to have listened to the weather forecast to see if it would clear today. What's the time, Julian?'

'Just gone eight,' said Julian. 'We *are* sleepy these days! Well, it's not raining so very hard now – let's see if the girls are awake, and put on our anoraks and go and wash at the spring.'

They all had breakfast – not quite as cheerful as usual, because it was a bit of a crowd in the tent and not nearly as much fun as having it in the sunshine. Still, the day might clear, and then they could go down to see Toby at the farm.

'I suppose we'd better go and explore those caves this morning,' said Dick, after breakfast. 'There's nothing else to do, and I refuse to play cards all morning.'

'We *all* refuse!' said George. 'Let's put on our coats and see if we can find the caves.'

'We can look at the map,' said Julian. 'It's a large-scale one. There must be a road or lane to them – they're quite well known. They're probably round the hill – a bit lower down.'

'Well, never mind – we'll see if we can find them, and if we can't it won't matter. We'll have been for a walk!' said Dick.

They set off in a fine drizzle, walking through the damp heather, Timmy leaping in front.

'Everyone got torches?' said Dick suddenly. 'I've got mine. We'll need them in the caves!'

Yes, everyone had a torch – except Timmy of course, and he, as Anne pointed out, had eyes that were far better for seeing in the dark than any torch could ever be!

They made their way down the hill and then veered off to the north side – and came suddenly upon a wide, rather chalky path, where the heather had been cut well back.

'This looks as if it leads somewhere,' said Julian, stopping.

'It might lead to an old chalk quarry,' said Dick, kicking some loose white lumps of chalk. 'Like the one near Kirrin.'

'Well, let's follow it up and see,' said George, and they went along it, kicking the lumps of chalk as they went. They rounded a corner and saw a notice.

To Billycock Caves

Warning

Keep only to the roped ways.

Beware of losing your way in the

unroped tunnels.

'This sounds good,' said Julian. 'Let's see – what did Toby tell us about the caves?'

'They're thousands of years old – they've got stalagmites and stalactites,' said George.

'Oh – I know what those are,' said Anne. 'They look like icicles hanging from the roof – and below, on the floor of the cave, other icicles seem to grow upwards to meet them!'

'Yes – the roof ones are stalac*tites* and the ground ones are stalag*mites*,' said Dick.

'I can *never* remember which is which,' said Anne.

'It's easy!' said Julian. 'The stalac*tite* icicles have to hold *tight* to the roof – and the stalag*mite* ones *might* some day join with the ones above them!'

The others laughed.

'I'll never forget which are which now,' said Anne.

The path they were following altered as they came near to the caves, and lost its chalky look. Just in front of the entrance the way was properly paved, and was no longer rough. The entrance was only about two metres high, and had over it a white board with two words painted very large in black.

BILLYCOCK CAVES

The warning they had read on the first notice they had come to was repeated on another one just inside the entrance. 'Read it, Tim,' said George, seeing him looking at it. 'And keep close to us!'

They went right in, and had to switch on their torches at once. Timmy was amazed to see the walls around him glittering suddenly in the light of the four torches. He began to bark, and the noise echoed all around in a very weird manner.

Timmy didn't like it, and he pressed close to George. She laughed. 'Come on, silly. These are only caves. You've been in plenty in your life, Timmy! Oh, don't they feel cold! I'm glad of my anorak!'

They passed through one or two small and ordinary caves and then came to a magnificent one, full of what looked like gleaming icicles. Some hung down from the roof, others rose up from the ground. In some places the one below had reached to the one hanging down, so that they had joined, making it look as if the cave was held up by great shining pillars.

'Oh!' said Anne, catching her breath. 'What a wonderful sight! How they gleam and shine!'

'It reminds me of cathedrals I've seen,' said Julian, looking up at the roof of the cave. 'I don't know why. All these beautiful pillars . . . come on, let's go into the next cave.'

The next one was smaller, but contained some wonderful coloured 'icicles' that shone and gleamed in the light of the torches.

'It's like a cave in Fairyland,' said Anne. 'Full of rainbow colours!'

The following cave had no colour, but was of a dazzling white, walls, roof, floor and pillars. So many stalactites and stalagmites had joined that they almost formed a snow-white screen through which the children peered – only to see even more of the strange 'icicles'.

They came to a threefold forking of the ways. The centre one was roped, but the other two tunnels were not. The children looked down the unroped tunnels, stretching away so dark and quiet, and shivered. How awful to go down one and lose the way, never to be found again, perhaps!

'Let's go down the roped way,' said George. 'Just to see where it leads to – more caves, probably.'

Timmy ran sniffing down one of the other ways, and George called him, 'Tim! You'll get lost! Come back.'

But Timmy didn't come back. He ran off into the darkness and the others felt cross.

'What's he after?' said Dick. 'TIM! TIM!' The echoes took up the last word and sent it repeatedly up and down the passage.

Timmy barked in answer, and at once the place was full of weird barking, echoing everywhere and making Anne put her fingers to her ears.

'Woof-oof-oof-oof!' said the echoes, sounding as if a gang of dogs were barking madly in the caves. Then Timmy appeared in the light of their torches, looking extremely surprised at the enormous noise he had created with his barking.

'I'll put you on the lead, Timmy,' scolded George. 'Keep to heel now. Surely you understand what that word means after all these years?'

Timmy did. He kept faithfully to heel as the little company went along a narrow, roped tunnel and came out into a succession of dazzling caves, all linked together by little passages or tunnels. They kept only to those that were roped. Many of them were not, and the Five longed to see where they led to, but were sensible enough not to try.

And then, as they were examining what looked like a frozen pool, which reflected the snowy roof above like a mirror, a strange noise came to their ears. They straightened themselves and listened.

It was a whistling sound, high-pitched and shrill, that filled the cave, and filled their eardrums, too, until they felt like bursting. It rose high, then died down – then rose again till the children were forced to put their hands to their heads – and died away.

Timmy couldn't bear it. He barked frantically and ran round and round like a mad thing. And then the second noise began – a howling! A howling that seemed to be tossed to and fro, and grew louder as the echoes threw it about from cave to cave! Anne clutched Dick, terrified.

'What is it?' she said. 'Quick, let's go!'

And, led by an extremely scared Timmy, the Five raced out of Billycock Caves as if a hundred dogs were after them!

13 A dreadful shock

The Five stood panting outside the entrance of the caves, feeling decidedly sheepish at having run away from a noise.

'Whew!' said Julian, mopping his forehead. 'That was very weird. That whistling – it got inside my head. It was like a – like a police whistle gone mad or something. As for the howling . . . well.'

'It was horrible,' said Anne, looking quite pale. 'Like wild animals. I'm not going into those caves again for anything. Let's get back to the camp.'

They walked soberly down the chalk-strewn path that led away from the caves and made their way back to their camp. The rain had stopped now, and the clouds were beginning to break.

The Five sat down inside a tent, and discussed the matter.

'We'll ask Toby if it's normal to hear noises like that,' said Dick. 'I wonder anyone ever visits the cave if it *is* infested with horrible whistles and screeches like that.'

'All the same, we were a bit cowardly,' said Julian, now feeling rather ashamed of himself.

'Well, go back and do a bit of howling yourself,' suggested George. 'It may frighten the howler as much as his howling scared *you*.'

'Not a chance,' said Julian promptly. 'I'm not going in for any howling matches.' He burrowed down under the rug for his binoculars and slung them round his neck.

'I'm going to have a look at the airfield,' he said. 'Just to see if I can spot Cousin Jeff.' He put the binoculars to his eyes and focused them on the airfield below them. He gave a sudden exclamation.

'There's quite a lot going on at the airfield this morning!' he said in surprise. 'Dozens of people there! I wonder what's up. There are quite a lot of planes, too – they must all have arrived this morning!'

Each of the others took a turn at looking through the binoculars. Yes – Julian was right. There was certainly something going on at the airfield today. Men hurried about, and then came the noise of yet another aeroplane, which zoomed neatly down to the runway.

'Oh – *another* plane!' said Dick. 'Where did all the others come from? We never heard them.'

'They must have arrived while we were in the caves,' said Julian. 'I wish we could ask Toby's Cousin Jeff what all the excitement is about.'

'We could go down to the farm after our lunch and see if he's heard anything,' suggested Anne, and the others agreed.

'Oh good, the sun's coming out again,' said George, as a shaft of warm sunlight burst out from behind a cloud, and the sun sailed into a patch of blue sky. 'The heather will soon dry now. Let's have the news on – we may just catch the weather forecast. I don't want to carry my anorak about if it's going to clear up.'

They switched on the little radio – but they had missed the weather news. 'How annoying,' said Dick and raised his hand to switch off – and then he heard two words that stopped him. They were 'Billycock Hill'! He left his hand suspended in the air and listened, full of surprise. The announcer's voice came clearly to the fore.

'The aeroplanes stolen from Billycock Hill

airfield were two valuable ones, into which had been incorporated new devices,' said the voice from the radio. 'It is possible that they were stolen because of these. We regret that it appears that two of our best pilots flew them away – Flight-Lieutenant Jeffrey Thomas and Flight-Lieutenant Ray Wells. No news has been received of either plane. Both disappeared during a storm over Billycock Hill during the night.'

There was a pause, and then the announcer went on to another item of news. Dick switched off the radio and looked blankly at the others. No one had a word to say at first.

'To think that *Jeff* could do a thing like that – Jeff a traitor – flying off with a plane of ours to sell to an enemy!' said Julian at last, voicing the thought of all the others.

'We heard the planes go!' said Dick. 'Two of them. We ought to go to the police and tell what we know. Not that it's much. But imagine JEFF doing that! I liked him so much.'

'So did I,' said Anne, turning her head away.

'So did Timmy,' said George. 'And he hardly ever makes a mistake about anyone.'

'What will poor Toby do?' said Dick. 'He

thought the world of Jeff.'

Timmy suddenly ran off a few yards and began barking – a welcoming bark this time. Julian looked to see who was coming. It was Toby!

He came up to them and sat down beside them. He looked pale and shocked, although he tried to smile at them.

'I've got awful news,' he said in a funny, croaking voice.

'We know,' said Dick. 'We've just heard it on the radio. Oh, Toby – *Jeff*!'

To everyone's horror Toby's face crumpled up and tears poured down his cheeks. He made no attempt to wipe them away; indeed, he hardly seemed to know that they were there. Nobody knew what to do – except Timmy. He scrambled over Julian and very sympathetically licked Toby's wet face, whining as he did so. Toby put his arm round the dog's neck and began to speak.

'It *wasn't* Jeff! Jeff couldn't have done such a thing. He couldn't! You know he couldn't, don't you?' He turned quite fiercely on the others as he spoke.

'*I* can't believe that he did,' said Julian. 'He

seemed to me to be absolutely honest and trustworthy, even though I only met him that once.'

'He was – well – a sort of hero to me,' said Toby, beginning to mop his cheeks with his hanky, and staring in surprise to see it so damp. 'Oh, I'm being silly to go on like this! But when the military police came to our farm this morning to ask questions about Jeff – he's my dad's nephew, you know – I couldn't believe my ears. I was so furious with one that I yelled at him – and Mum sent me out of the room.'

'I suppose both Jeff and the other man have definitely *gone*?' asked Julian. 'No other pilots are missing, are they?'

'No, I asked that,' said Toby dismally. 'Everyone answered roll-call at the camp this morning except Jeff and Ray. Ray is Jeff's best friend, you know.'

'It looks bad,' said Dick, after a long pause.

'But it's *not true* that Jeff's a traitor!' cried Toby, up in arms again. 'Are you suggesting that he is?'

'No, I'm not,' said Dick. 'I don't—' Then he stopped as Timmy ran off and barked fiercely.

Now who was coming?

A deep voice called to Timmy. 'Down, boy, down! Where are your friends?'

Julian scrambled up and saw two military policemen standing facing the excited Timmy.

'Here, Tim,' called Julian. 'It's all right. Friends!'

Timmy ran to him and the two burly men came up.

'You the children camping on this hill?' asked the first one. 'Well, we want to ask you a few questions about last night. You were here then, weren't you?'

'Yes. We know what you've come about, too,' said Julian. 'We'll tell you all we know – but we're pretty certain that Flight-Lieutenant Thomas didn't have anything to do with it.'

'That's as may be,' said the man. 'Well, sit down, all of you, and we'll have a little talk.'

Soon they were sitting down in the heather, while Julian told all they knew, which wasn't much – just the sound of the two aeroplanes flying off together.

'And you heard nothing suspicious last night – nothing at all?' asked the first man.

'Nothing,' said Julian.

'Nobody about at all, I suppose?' asked the second man, looking up from his notebook in which he'd been writing.

'Oh – well, yes – there were people about,' said Julian, suddenly remembering the butterfly man, Mr Brent, who had said that he and Mr Gringle were out looking at their moth-traps.

The first policeman asked some rapid questions and Julian and the others told them what little they knew – although Julian knew the most, of course.

'You're sure it was Mr Brent you saw?' asked the policeman.

'Well – he *said* he was,' said Julian. 'And he carried a butterfly net on his shoulder – and he wore the same dark glasses I saw him wearing earlier. Of course, it was pretty dark – but I honestly *think* it was Mr Brent. I didn't see or hear Mr Gringle. Mr Brent said he was some way off. They're both mad on moth and butterfly hunting.'

'I see,' said the policeman, and the second one shut his notebook. 'Thanks very much. I think we'll just go and pay a call on these – er – what do you call them – butterfly men? Where do they hang out?'

The children offered to guide them on their way, and they all went with the two burly men almost to the butterfly farm.

'Well, thanks a lot,' said the first policeman as they came near the tumbledown cottage. 'We'll go on alone, now. You get back to your camp.'

'Will you send us word as soon as you know it wasn't my Cousin Jeff?' asked Toby, forlornly. 'He'll be getting in touch with you, I know, as soon as he hears what he's suspected of.'

'It's bad luck on you, son – he's your cousin, isn't he?' said the big policeman kindly. 'But you'll have to accept it – it was Jeff Thomas all right that flew off in one of those aeroplanes last night. There's no doubt about it!'

14 Mr Gringle is annoyed

The military police went off down the hill to the butterfly farm, and the five children stood disconsolately watching them, with Timmy staring, too, tail well down. He didn't quite know what had happened but he was sure it was something dreadful . . .

'Well – it's no good waiting about here, I suppose,' said Julian. 'I bet the police won't get anything useful out of the butterfly men – *they* wouldn't have noticed anything when they were out last night, except their precious moths!'

They were just turning away when they heard someone screaming in a high voice, and they stopped to listen in surprise.

'It must be Mrs Janes,' said Dick. 'What's up with her?'

'We'd better see,' said Julian, and he and the others, with Timmy at their heels, went quickly down to the cottage. They heard the voices of the two policemen as they came near.

'Now, now, Madam, don't get so upset!' one was saying in a kindly voice. 'We've only come to ask a few questions.'

'Go away, go away!' screamed the woman, and actually battered at the men with her little bony hands. 'Why are you here? Go away, I tell you!'

'Now listen, calm down!' said the other man patiently. 'We want to talk to Mr Gringle and Mr Brent – are they here?'

'Who? Who did you say? Oh, them! They're out with their nets,' mumbled the woman. 'I'm all alone here, and I'm scared of strangers. You go away.'

'Listen,' said one policeman. 'Were Mr Gringle and Mr Brent out on the hills last night?'

'I'm in my bed at night,' she answered. 'How would *I* know? You go away and leave me in peace.'

The policemen looked at one another, and shook their heads. It was clearly useless to find out anything from this frightened old woman.

'Well, we'll go, Madam,' said one, patting her shoulder gently. 'Sorry we've scared you –

there's nothing to be afraid of.'

They turned away and came back up the slope of the hill, seeing the children standing silently there.

'We heard old Mrs Janes screaming,' said Julian. 'So we came to see what was happening.'

'The butterfly men, as you call them, are out with their nets,' said one policeman. 'A funny life – catching insects and looking after their eggs and caterpillars. Well – I don't suppose they know anything about last night's job. Not that there's anything to know! Two pilots flew off with the planes, we know who they were – and that's that!'

'Well, one was NOT my Cousin Jeff,' said Toby, fiercely. The men shrugged their shoulders and went off together.

The five children went off up the hill again, very silent. 'I think we'd better have something to eat,' said Julian at last. 'We've had no lunch – and it's long past our usual time. Toby, stay and have some with us.'

'I couldn't eat a thing,' said Toby. 'Not a thing!'

'Let's get out what we've got,' said Julian,

and they all went to the little 'larder'. Nobody really felt like eating – but when the food was there, in front of them, they found that they were quite hungry – except poor Toby, who sat forlorn and pale-faced, trying to chew through a sandwich, but not making a very good job of it!

Timmy began to bark in the middle of the meal, and everyone looked to see who was coming now. Julian thought he saw a movement some way down the hill, and took his binoculars and put them to his eyes.

'I *think* it's Mr Gringle,' he said. 'I can see his net too. He's out butterflying, I suppose.'

'Let's shout to him,' said Dick. 'We can tell him why the police went to call at his cottage this morning, when he wasn't there. He'll never get any sense out of Mrs Janes.'

Julian called out, and there came an answering call.

'He's coming up,' said Dick.

Timmy ran to meet him, and soon the man was just below them, panting as he made his way up the steep slope.

'I hoped I'd see you,' he said. 'I want you to

look out for some special moths for me – another day-flying one like the Six-Spot Burnet you saw the other day. It's the Cinnabar moth – it's got rich crimson underwings, and – and—'

'Yes – I know that one,' said Julian. 'We'll look out for it. We just wanted to tell you that two military policemen went to your cottage a little while ago to ask you some questions about last night – and we're sure Mrs Janes won't be able to explain anything to you, so we thought we'd better tell you ourselves.'

Mr Gringle looked absolutely blank and bewildered. 'But – but why on earth should military policemen come to our cottage?' he said at last.

'For nothing much,' said Julian. 'Only to ask you if you saw anything suspicious when you were out looking at your moth-traps last night – you see, two aeroplanes were—'

Mr Gringle interrupted in a very surprised voice. 'But – but, dear boy, I wasn't out at all last night! It wouldn't have been a bit of good looking for moths anywhere, on our moth-traps or anywhere else, on a night like that.'

'Well,' said Julian, also surprised, 'I saw your

friend Mr Brent, and he *said* you were both out looking at your moth-traps.'

Mr Gringle stared at Julian as if he were mad, and his mouth fell open in amazement. 'Mr *Brent*!' he said at last. 'But Peter – that's Mr Brent – was at home with *me*! We were busy writing up our notes together.'

There was a silence after this surprising statement. Julian frowned. What was all this? Was Mr Gringle trying to hide the fact that he and his friend had been out on the hills the night before?

'Well – I definitely saw Mr Brent,' said Julian at last. 'It was very dark, I admit – but I'm sure I saw his butterfly net – and his dark glasses.'

'He doesn't *wear* dark glasses,' said Mr Gringle, still more astonished. 'What *is* this tale? Is it a joke of some sort? If you can't talk better sense than this, I'm going.'

'Wait!' said Dick, something else occurring to him. 'You say that Mr Brent doesn't wear dark glasses – then who was the man that took the moth from us yesterday evening about six o'clock and gave us some money? He *said* he was Mr Brent, your colleague!'

'This is all nonsense!' said Mr Gringle, getting up angrily. 'Wasting my time on a silly joke like this! Brent doesn't wear dark glasses, I tell you – and he wasn't at home at six o'clock yesterday – we'd been to buy some tackle in the next town. He was with *me*, not at the cottage. You couldn't possibly have seen him! What do you mean by all this nonsense – dark glasses, money for a moth – and seeing Brent on the hillside last night when he didn't stir out of the house!'

He was now standing up, looking very fierce, his bright eyes flashing behind his thick glasses.

'Well,' said Julian, 'all this is very puzzling, and—'

'Puzzling! You're nothing but a pack of nitwitted, ill-mannered children!' suddenly roared Mr Gringle, losing his temper. Timmy gave a warning growl, and stood up – he didn't allow anyone to shout at his friends!

Mr Gringle went off angrily, trampling down the heather as if he were trampling down the children. They heard him muttering to himself as he went off. They looked at one another in really great surprise.

'Well – I don't know what to make of all this!' said Julian helplessly. 'Was I dreaming last night? No – I *did* see that man – half see him, anyway – and he *did* say he was Mr Brent, and that Gringle was somewhere near. But – if he wasn't Brent, who was he? And what was he doing on a stormy night, hunting moths?'

Nobody could make even a guess. Toby spoke first.

'Perhaps the man you saw was mixed up in the stealing of those aeroplanes – you never know?'

'Impossible, Toby!' said Julian. 'That's *too* far-fetched. I can't say that I understand it at all – but honestly, he didn't seem like a man who could steal an aeroplane!'

'Who was the man that gave us the money then, if he wasn't Brent?' said Dick, puzzled.

'Could it have been Mrs Janes's son, pretending he was Brent – just for a silly joke?' said George.

'What was he like?' asked Toby at once. 'I know Will Janes – I told you he's often been to our farm. We don't have him now because he drinks so much and he isn't reliable any more. What was this man Brent like? I'd soon know if he was Will Janes pretending to be someone else!'

'He was small and thin, with dark glasses,' began Dick – and Toby interrupted him at once.

'Then it wasn't Will Janes! He's tall and burly – with a thick neck and, anyway, he doesn't wear dark glasses – or any glasses at all!'

'Then who on earth was it? And WHY did he pretend to be Brent, Gringle's colleague?' wondered Dick. Everyone frowned and puzzled over the whole thing – but nobody could think of a sensible reason for anyone wanting to pretend to be Mr Brent!

'Let's get on with our food,' said George at last. 'We stopped in the middle of it – and the rest is still waiting for us. Have another ham sandwich, Julian?'

They all munched in silence, thinking hard. Toby sighed. 'I don't really feel that this mix-up with the butterfly men and somebody else, whoever he is, has anything to do with the stealing of the aeroplanes. I wish it had!'

'All the same – it wants looking into,' said Dick seriously. 'And what's more – I vote we keep our eyes and ears open. *Something's* going on at the butterfly farm!'

15 More news – and a night trip

The Five spent most of the afternoon talking about the mystery of the man who had pretended to be Mr Brent. It really was difficult to understand why anyone would do such a foolish thing, especially as it could be so easily found out.

'I can only think there's a madman about who has got it into his head that he's Mr Brent!' said Dick at last. 'No wonder he didn't seem to recognise that butterfly we took him!'

'Do you know what I think would be a good idea?' suddenly said George. 'Why don't we slip down to the butterfly farm tonight, when it's getting dark, and see if the false Mr Brent is there, *and* the real one – whom we've never seen, by the way – *and* Mr Gringle?'

'Hmm – yes – quite an idea,' said Julian, seriously. 'But only Dick and I will go.'

'I'll come, too,' said Toby.

'Right,' said Julian. 'But we'll have to be really

careful – because if there *is* something funny going on down there, we don't want to be caught. It wouldn't be very pleasant!'

'Take Timmy with you,' said George at once.

'No. He might bark or something,' said Dick. 'We'll be all right, George. We've had enough adventures by now to teach us how to go about things like this! Ha – I'll look forward to tonight!'

Everyone suddenly felt much more cheerful, even Toby. He managed a very small smile, and stood up to brush the crumbs off his jumper.

'I'm going now,' he said. 'I've a lot of farm jobs to do this afternoon – I'll meet you at the big oak tree behind the butterfly farm – did you notice it?'

'Yes – an enormous one,' said Julian. 'Right. Be there at – say – ten o'clock. No, eleven – it'll be dark by then, or almost.'

'See you there!' said Toby and plunged down the hill, accompanied for a little way by Timmy.

'Well – I feel much better now we've made a definite plan,' said Dick. 'Look, it's half past five already! *Don't* suggest tea, George – we had our lunch so late!'

'I wasn't going to,' said George. 'We'll miss it out and have a really good supper later on. And don't let's forget to listen to the news at six o'clock – there *might* be something about Jeff and his friend Ray – and the aeroplanes.'

So, just before six o'clock, they switched on the little radio, and listened intently for the news. It came at last – and almost the first piece was about the stolen aeroplanes. The children listened, holding their breath, bending close to the radio.

'The two aeroplanes stolen from Billycock airfield last night, flown away by Flight-Lieutenant Jeffrey Thomas and Flight-Lieutenant Ray Wells, have been found. Both planes apparently crashed into the sea, but were seen, and there is a chance of their being salvaged. The pilots were not found, and are presumed to have been drowned. At Edinburgh this afternoon there was a grand rally of—'

Julian switched off the news and looked at the others soberly. 'Well – that's that! Crashed, both of them! That was because of the storm, I suppose. Well, at least no enemy will be able to get hold of the new devices that were in the planes.'

'But – that means Toby's cousin is drowned –

or killed,' said Anne, her face very white.

'Yes. But remember, if he flew away in that plane, he was a traitor,' said Dick gravely.

'But Toby's cousin didn't *seem* like a traitor,' said George. 'He seemed so – well, so *very* honest, and I can't say anything better than that. I feel as if I'll never trust my judgment of anyone again. I liked him so much.'

'So did I,' said Dick, frowning. 'Well, these things happen – but I just wish it hadn't been Toby's cousin. He was such a hero to him. I don't feel as if Toby will ever be quite the same after this – it's something so absolutely *horrible*!'

Nobody said anything for a little while. They were all profoundly shocked – not only by the idea of Cousin Jeff being a traitor, but also by the news that he had been drowned. It seemed such a horrible end to come to that bright-eyed smiling young airman they had joked with only the other day.

'Do you think we ought to pack up and go home?' said Anne. 'I mean – won't it be awkward for the Thomases to have us hanging around when they must feel shocked and unhappy?'

'No, we don't need to bother them much at the

farm,' said Julian. 'And I don't think we can desert Toby at the moment. It'll help him to have friends around, you know.'

'Yes. You're right,' said Dick. 'This is the sort of time to have good friends – poor Toby. He'll be knocked out by this last piece of news.'

'Will he be waiting for you at the old oak tree tonight, do you think?' asked George.

'Don't know,' said Julian. 'It doesn't matter if he's not there, anyway – Dick and I can do all the snooping around that's necessary. And it'll take our minds off this shock a bit – to try and solve the mystery down at the butterfly farm!'

They went for a walk round the hill, with Timmy leaping over the heather in delight. He couldn't understand the lack of laughter and the unusual solemnity shown by his four friends, and he was pleased to be able to forget any troubles and sniff for rabbits.

They had their suppers at eight o'clock and then turned on the radio to listen to a programme. 'We'll hear the news at nine,' said Dick. 'Just in *case* there might be any more.'

But the nine o'clock news only repeated what had been said about the two planes in the six o'clock broadcast, and not a word more. Dick switched off and gazed down at the airfield below.

There were still quite a lot of planes there, although some of them had taken off and flown away during the day. Julian trained his binoculars on the field.

'Not so many men scurrying about now,' he said. 'Things are quietening down. What a shock it must have been for everyone there last night, to hear the planes revved up, and then flown away! They *must* have been amazed!'

'Maybe they didn't hear them go, in the storm,' said George.

'They must have,' said Dick. '*We* heard them up here. Well, what about you girls turning in? Dick and I don't want to, in case we fall off to sleep – we've got to slip away about half past ten or we won't be down at the oak tree at eleven.'

'I wish you'd take Timmy with you,' said George uneasily. 'I don't *like* the butterfly farm – or the witch-like woman there – or the man you met with dark glasses who wasn't Mr Brent, or the son you haven't seen.'

'Don't be silly, George,' said Julian. 'We'll be

back by twelve, I expect – and Timmy's sure to bark in welcome, so you'll know we're safe.'

The girls wouldn't go to their tent to sleep, so they all sat and talked, and watched the sun slip behind the clear horizon. The weather was now perfect again, and there wasn't a cloud in the sky. It was difficult to imagine the sweeping rain and howling wind of last night's storm.

'Well,' said Julian at last, looking at his watch. 'Time we went. Timmy, look after the girls as usual.'

'Woof,' said Timmy, understanding perfectly.

'And you look after *your*selves,' said Anne. 'We'll come down a little way with you – it's such a lovely evening.'

They all set off together, and the girls went halfway to the butterfly farm and then turned back with Timmy. 'Well, Tim – mind you bark at twelve, when they come back,' said Anne. 'Although somehow I think that both George and I will still be awake!'

The two boys went on down the hill and round to the right across towards the butterfly farm. It was almost dark now, although the June night was very clear and bright.

'Better be careful we're not seen,' muttered Julian. 'It's such a clear night.'

They made their way to the big old oak tree that stood at the back of the butterfly farm. Toby wasn't there – but in about two minutes they heard a slight rustling noise, and saw Toby, panting a little, as if he had been hurrying. Then he was close beside them.

'Sorry I'm a bit late,' he whispered. 'Did you hear the six o'clock news?'

'Yes – we're awfully sorry about it,' said Julian.

'Well – as I still don't believe that Cousin Jeff stole the aeroplanes with Ray Wells, but that somebody else did, I wasn't any more upset than before,' said Toby. 'If Jeff didn't steal the plane, he wasn't in it when it crashed, so he's not drowned. See?'

'Yes. I see,' said Julian, glad that Toby had taken the news in that way, but convinced himself that there wasn't really much hope.

'What are your plans?' whispered Toby. 'There are lights in the cottage windows – and I don't think any curtains are pulled. We could go and peer into each one and see exactly who's there!'

'Good idea,' said Julian. 'Come on – and, *don't* make a noise. Single file, of course. I'll lead the way.'

And silently and slowly they went round the oak tree and down to the tumbledown cottage. What would they see there, when they looked through those lit windows?

16 Looking through windows

The three tiptoed quietly up to the cottage. 'Don't go too near when you look in,' whispered Julian. 'Keep a little distance away. We'll be able to see who's in the rooms, but they mustn't be able to see us outside. I really hope they won't!'

'Look in the downstairs rooms,' said Dick. 'See, that's the kitchen window over there. Mrs Janes may be there, if she's still up.'

They crept to the uncurtained window. The room was lit by only a candle, and was full of shadows. The boys gazed in.

Mrs Janes *was* there, sitting up in a brown rocking-chair, clad in a dirty dressing gown. She rocked herself to and fro, and although the boys couldn't see her face, they sensed that the old woman was frightened and unhappy. Her head was sunk on her chest, and when she put her wispy hair back from her face, her hand shook.

'She's no witch, poor thing!' whispered Dick,

feeling sad to see her rocking to and fro all by herself so late at night. 'She's just a poor frightened old woman.'

'Why is she up so late?' wondered Julian. 'She must be waiting for someone.'

'Yes. She might be. We'd better look out then,' said Toby at once, looking behind him as if he expected to see someone creeping up.

'Now let's go round to the front,' said Dick. So they tiptoed there, and saw another lit window – much more brightly lit than the kitchen window had been. They kept a little way from the pane, afraid of being seen. They looked in and saw two men there, sitting at a table, poring over some papers.

'Mr Gringle!' said Julian, in a low voice. 'No doubt about that – and the other one must be his colleague, Mr Brent, I suppose. He isn't wearing dark glasses, as that man was we gave the butterfly to and who gave us money. He isn't a *bit* like him!'

They all looked intently at the friend. He was a completely ordinary man, with a small moustache, dark hair and a rather big nose. Not at all like the 'Mr Brent' they had seen the day before.

'What are they doing?' whispered Toby.

'It looks as if they're making lists of something – probably making out bills for their customers,' said Julian. 'Anyway – they look completely ordinary sitting there, doing a completely ordinary job. I think Mr Gringle was speaking the truth when he said that it wasn't Mr Brent who gave us the money, and it certainly wasn't him either that I saw on the hillside last night with a butterfly net.'

'Then who *was* it?' asked Dick, pulling the others right away from the window, in order to talk more easily. 'And why did he carry the butterfly net and tell that lie about moth-traps? Why was he on the hill, the night the planes were stolen?'

'Yes – why *was* he? I'd like to ask him that!' said Toby in too loud a voice. The others nudged him at once, and he spoke more softly. 'Something funny was going on last night – something people don't know anything about. I'd like to find that phony Mr Brent you met on the hillside, Julian!'

'Well, maybe we will,' said Julian. 'Now – any other window lit? Yes – one up there, under the roof. Who's there, I wonder?'

'Perhaps it's Mrs Janes's son,' said Dick. 'It'd be just like him to take one of the three bedrooms and make her sleep downstairs in the old rocking-chair! I expect the other two little rooms up there are used by the butterfly men.'

'How can we see into the lit room?' wondered Toby. 'Look – if we got up in that tree there, we'd see in.'

'There's an easier way!' said Julian, switching his torch on and off very quickly, giving the others just half a second to see a ladder leaning against a nearby woodshed.

'Good – yes, that'd be much easier,' said Dick. 'But we'll have to be really quiet. Whoever's in there would come to the window at once if he so much as heard the top of the ladder grating against the window ledge!'

'Well, we'll manage it all right,' said Julian. 'The window isn't very high, and the ladder isn't very heavy. Between us we can place it very gently against the wall without disturbing anyone!'

The ladder was certainly quite light. The boys found no difficulty in carrying it slowly and carefully across to the cottage. They placed it against the wall without a sound.

'I'll go up,' whispered Julian. 'Hold the ladder steady – and keep a lookout! Give me a signal if you hear anything at all, because I don't want to be trapped at the top of the ladder!'

The others held the sides as he climbed the rather rickety rungs. He came to the lit window and very cautiously and slowly lifted his head until he could see right into the room.

It was lit by a candle, a very small and untidy room, poorly furnished. A man sat on the bed there, a big hulking man, with broad shoulders and a neck like a bull. Julian gazed at him – yes, that must be Mrs Janes's son, who, she said, was so unkind to her. Julian remembered the mumbling voice saying that her son was cruel. 'He hits me. He twists my arm!' Yes, the man on the bed could be a nasty bully, no doubt about that.

He was reading a newspaper close to the candle.

As Julian looked at him, he pulled out a big watch from his pocket and stared at it, muttering something that Julian couldn't hear. He stood up, and the boy was so afraid that he might come to the window, that he slithered down the ladder as quickly as possible.

'The son's in there,' he whispered to the others. 'I was afraid he was coming to the window to look out; that's why I slid down so quickly. Ouch! I've got a splinter in the palm of my hand doing that! Toby – could you creep up to the top in a minute or two and look in – just to make sure I'm right, and that it *is* Will Janes, the old woman's son?'

Toby went up the ladder as soon as they were certain that Will Janes wasn't going to look out. He came down almost at once.

'Yes – that's Will – but he's *really* changed!' whispered Toby. 'He looks like a thug now – and yet he was a kind decent man not so long ago. Mum said he'd fallen in with some bad men, and had taken to drinking – I suppose he's different now.'

'He looked at his watch as if he was expecting someone,' said Julian. 'I wonder – now, I wonder – if the man who paraded about the hillside last night with a net is coming here tonight? I'd like to get a good look at him. He can't be up to any good.'

'Well – let's hide somewhere and wait,' suggested Toby. 'Nobody knows I've slipped out to be with you, so I won't be missed. Anyway, Mum wouldn't mind if she knew I was on a night trip with you two!'

'We'll hide in that barn over there,' said Julian, and, on tiptoe again, they crossed to an old ruined barn, whose roof was partly off, and whose walls were falling in. It smelt dirty and there seemed no clean place to sit in, but at last Julian pulled out some dusty sacks and laid them in a corner and they sat there waiting in the dark.

'Ugh!' said Dick. 'What a horrible smell in here – old rotting potatoes, or something. I wish we'd chosen somewhere else.'

'Shh!' said Julian suddenly, giving him a nudge that made him jump. 'I can hear something.'

They all sat silent and listened. They could certainly hear something – yes – quiet footsteps, very quiet – made by rubber-soled shoes. The soft sounds passed by the barn, and they could no longer hear them. Then came a soft, low whistle.

Julian stood up and looked through the broken barn window. 'I think there are two men standing below Will Janes's bedroom,' he whispered. 'They must be the men he was waiting for. He'll be coming down. I hope they don't come into this barn to talk!'

This was a horrible thought, but there was no chance of going anywhere else, because at that moment the front door opened and Will Janes came out. Julian, still looking through the broken pane, could see him dimly outlined in the light that came from Mr Gringle's front window.

The three men went off very quietly round the cottage. 'Come on,' said Julian. 'Let's shadow them. We might hear something to explain what's going on.'

'What's the time?' asked Dick. 'I hope the girls won't start worrying about us. It must be gone twelve by now.'

'Yes. It is,' said Julian, looking at the luminous hands of his watch. 'It can't be helped. They'll guess we're on to something!'

They crept after the three men, who went to a clump of trees on the other side of the glasshouses. There they began to talk, but in such low tones that the three boys could hear nothing but the murmur of the voices.

Then one man raised his voice. It was Will Janes – Toby recognised it at once and told the others. 'It's Will. He's furious about something.

He always loses his temper when he thinks people have treated him badly in any way – and it sounds as if he thinks those two men have.'

The two men tried to quiet him, but he wouldn't be pacified.

'I want my money!' the boys heard him say. 'I helped you, didn't I. I hid you here, didn't I, till the job was done. Then give me my money!'

His voice rose almost to a shout, and the two men with him grew frightened. Exactly what happened next the boys never knew, but suddenly there was the sound of a blow and a fall – then another blow and a fall – Will Janes laughed. It wasn't a nice laugh.

In a few seconds there came an anxious voice from the window of the room where Mr Gringle and his friend were at work. 'Who's there? What's happening?'

CRASH! That was the sound of breaking glass! Will Janes had picked up a big stone and flung it at the nearby glasshouse. It made the three boys almost jump out of their skins.

'It's all right! I came out to see who was prowling about!' shouted Will Janes. 'And whoever it was has broken some of the glass in your butterfly house. I've been out here shouting, trying to catch him.'

He came blundering towards the house – and then, as luck would have it, his torch picked out the three crouching boys. He gave a yell!

'Who's this? Here they are, kids who've been trying to smash the glass! Catch them – that's right – I've got two of them – you catch the third!'

17 Quite a lot happens

Things then happened so quickly that, to their utter amazement, the three boys found themselves captives, unable to escape.

Big Will Janes had hold of both Dick and Toby – and he was so strong, and held them in such a vice-like grip, one in each hand, that it was hopeless to try to get away.

Julian had run straight into Mr Gringle and Mr Brent, and the men had captured him between them. They were very angry.

'What do you mean by coming here and snooping around, smashing our glasshouses!' yelled Mr Gringle, shaking Julian in his rage. 'We'll lose all our butterflies through that broken pane!'

'Let me go. We didn't break your glass,' shouted Julian.

'He did! I saw him!' shouted Will Janes.

'You didn't!' cried Toby. 'Let me go, Will. I'm

Toby Thomas, from Billycock Farm. You let me go or my dad'll have something to say!'

'Oho – so it's Toby Thomas, is it?' said Will in a sneering voice. 'Toby Thomas, whose dad won't employ Will Janes now because he turns his nose up at him. You wait till I tell the police tomorrow what I've caught you doing – I'll say you're the kids that have been taking our hens!'

Will dragged the angry boys over to a shed, calling out to the other two men. 'Bring them here. Chuck them in and we'll lock the door and let them cool off till tomorrow morning!'

Julian struggled valiantly against the two men, but short of kicking them viciously there was nothing he could do to escape – and he didn't really want to harm them. It was all a mistake!

And then – oh, joy – there came a sound that made Julian's heart leap – the bark of a dog!

'Timmy! It's Timmy!' yelled Julian to the others. 'Call him! He'll soon make Janes drop you!'

'Tim, Tim!' shouted Dick, and Timmy ran to him at once, and began to growl so ferociously that Will Janes stopped dragging the boys to the shed.

'Set us free or he'll spring at you,' warned Dick. Timmy growled again, and nipped Will's ankle just to let him know he had teeth. Will let both boys go, and they staggered away from him in relief. Then Timmy ran to Julian – but Mr Gringle and Mr Brent had already heard his fierce growls and didn't wait for any more! They gave Julian a shove away from them, and retreated into the cottage.

Will Janes also went into the cottage and lumbered up the stairs. The boys saw his figure outlined against the candlelight.

'Well, thank goodness he didn't go and scare his poor old mum,' said Julian, shaking his clothes straight. They had been twisted and pulled in the struggle. 'We'd better go and see if Will knocked those two men out – what a night! Good old Timmy – you just came in time!'

'I bet the girls sent him after us when twelve o'clock came,' said Dick. 'He'd smell our tracks easily. Now, go carefully – it's about here that Will floored those two men, whoever they were.'

But there was no sign of them at all. They must

have got up from the ground very quickly and made themselves scarce. 'They went while the going was good!' said Toby grimly. 'What do we do next?'

'Get back to the camp,' said Julian. 'We're really not much wiser now than when we came – except that we know that Gringle and Brent *are* butterfly men, and that Janes is a bad person and in with those two men he knocked out . . .'

'And that he helped them in some way, and hid them here – and hasn't been paid,' finished Dick. 'But how did he help them and why?'

'I've no idea,' said Julian. 'I can't think any more tonight – my mind just won't work. Go back home, Toby. We'll talk it all out tomorrow.'

Toby went off to the farm, puzzled and excited. What an evening! What would Cousin Jeff say when he told him – but no, he couldn't tell him. People said he had gone off in that plane, and that he was now at the bottom of the sea.

'But I won't believe it,' thought the tired boy, stoutly. 'I will – not – believe it!'

The girls were very relieved to hear the boys and Timmy coming back.

'What's happened? Why are you so late?' said

George. 'Timmy found you all right, of course?'

'Couldn't have come at a better moment,' said Julian, grinning in the light of George's torch. 'I suppose you sent him after us?'

'We did,' said George. 'He wanted to go, anyway. He kept whining and whining as if you needed help – so we sent him off.'

'And we *did* need help!' said Dick, flinging himself down in the heather. 'Listen to our tale!'

He and Julian told it, and the girls listened, astonished.

'What *has* been going on down there?' said George, puzzled. 'What has Will Janes been up to with those men? How can we find out?'

'*He* won't talk,' said Julian. 'Nobody can make him, either. But I think maybe if we went down tomorrow morning and found that he'd gone out, we might persuade Mrs Janes to tell us a few secrets.'

'Yes – that's a good idea,' said George. 'She *must* know what her son's been up to – especially if he's been hiding people there. She'd have to feed them of course. Yes – Mrs Janes would tell you – if she could!'

'But now,' said Julian, snuggling down in the

heather on his rug, 'now, you two gabblers, I want to go to sleep. Goodnight!'

'Well! *Who's* been doing the gabbling!' said George. 'We have hardly been able to get a word in! Come on, Anne – we can go to sleep all right now. I wonder if Toby's home safely, and fast asleep in bed!'

Yes, Toby was home, but he wasn't asleep! He was still brooding over his Cousin Jeff. If only he could *do* something – but he couldn't. Cousin Jeff had disappeared, and he, and he only, could clear himself of the terrible charge of traitor . . . but people said he was drowned.

Next morning the Five awoke late, even Timmy. There wasn't a great deal left in the larder, and Julian hoped that Toby would bring up some more food. If not, they would have to go down to Billycock Farm and get some. They breakfasted on bread and butter and cheese, with water to wash it down and a humbug from the tin to follow!

'We'll go straight down to the butterfly farm, I think,' said Julian, taking the leadership as he always did when there was any quick decision to be made. 'Dick, you'd better take on the asking of questions – the old lady was so touched when you gave her that money! She's probably got a soft spot for you now.'

'Right,' said Dick. 'Well, are we ready?'

They set off to the butterfly farm, Timmy at their heels. When they came near, they slowed their steps, not wanting to run into Will Janes. But there didn't seem to be anybody about at all, not even the butterfly men themselves.

'They've probably gone off butterfly-hunting, I should think,' said Dick. 'Look – there's poor Mrs Janes trying to peg up her washing – dropping half of it on the ground.'

Anne ran over to the little woman.

'I'll peg up the things for you,' she said. 'Here, let me have them.'

Mrs Janes turned to her and Anne was shocked to see that her right eye was black and bruised.

'How did you get that black eye?' she began. 'Here give me the whole basket. Oh, what a lot of washing!'

Mrs Janes seemed a little dazed. She let Anne peg up the things without a word – she just stood and watched her.

'Where are Mr Gringle and Mr Brent?' asked

Anne as she pegged.

Mrs Janes mumbled something. Anne made out with some difficulty that they had gone butterfly-hunting. 'And where's your son, Will?' she asked, having been prompted to ask this by signs from Julian.

To her dismay Mrs Janes began to sob. The woman lifted her dirty apron and covered her head with it, and then, half blinded by it, she stumbled towards the kitchen door, her arms stretched out in front of her.

'What's the matter with her this morning?' said Anne to the others.

Dick ran to the kitchen door and guided the old lady in, sitting her down in her rocking-chair. Her apron slid down from her head and she looked at him.

'You're the one that give me that money,' she mumbled, and patted his hand. 'Kind, you are. Nobody's kind to me now. My son's cruel. He hits me.'

'Did he give you that black eye?' asked Dick, gently. 'When? Today?'

'Yes. He wanted money – he always wants money,' wept Mrs Janes. 'And I wasn't going to give him that money. And he hit me. And then the police came and took him away.'

'What! The police took him – this morning do you mean?' asked Dick astonished.

The others came a little closer, astonished, too. It was only last night that Will Janes had captured two of them!

'They said he'd been thieving,' sobbed Mrs Janes. 'Robbed old Farmer Darvil of his ducks. But it's those bad men that changed my son. He was a good son once.'

'What men?' asked Dick, patting the skinny hand. 'You tell us everything. We understand. We'll help you.'

'You're the one that give me that money, aren't you?' she said once more. 'You'll help a poor old woman, won't you? It was those men, I tell you, that changed my son.'

'Where are they now? Did he hide them here?' asked Dick.

Mrs Janes clung to his hand and pulled him closer.

'There were four men,' she mumbled, in such a low voice that Dick could hardly hear. 'And my son, he was promised money if he hid them here, on Billycock Hill. They all had a secret, see? And they only talked about it when they were hiding up in my bedroom there – but I listened and I heard.'

'What was the secret?' asked Dick, his heart beating fast. Now perhaps he would hear what all this mystery was about.

'They were watching something,' whispered Mrs Janes. 'Watching something out on the hills. Sometimes daytime, sometimes night-time, always watching. And they hid up there in my little old room, and cook for them I did and got nothing for it. Bad men they were.'

She sobbed again, and the four children felt sad and embarrassed.

'Don't worry her any more,' said Anne.

Then there came the sound of feet outside and Mr Gringle walked by the window. He looked in and was astounded to see such a crowd in the little kitchen.

'What! You again!' he cried, when he saw Julian and Dick. 'You just look out! I told the police about you when they fetched Will Janes this morning. They'll be after *you* next, and you'll be punished for prowling round here at night and smashing my glasshouse! How *dare* you come here again!'

18 Nobody knows where to look

'Let's go,' said George. 'We can't find out any more from the poor old woman. I'm glad that son of hers has been arrested for thieving. At least he won't be here to knock her about any more!'

Mr Gringle began to talk angrily again, but the Five had had enough. Timmy growled and made him retreat.

'We're going, Mr Gringle,' said Julian coldly. 'We'll be very *glad* to see the police, if you've really sent them after us. Quite a lot has been going on here that you don't know anything about. You've noticed nothing but your butterflies and moths.'

'Anything wrong in that, you rude boy?' shouted Mr Gringle.

'Well, it would have been a good thing if you'd noticed how that man Janes knocked his poor mum about,' said Julian. 'I suppose you haven't even seen the bruised black eye she has this morning? No? I thought not. Well, maybe the police will be asking you a few questions soon – about the four strangers that have been hiding in that little bedroom up there!'

'What? What's that you say? What do you mean?' stammered Mr Gringle, astonished. 'Men? Where from? Who?'

'I've no idea,' said Julian. 'I wish I had.'

And then the Five walked off together, leaving a very puzzled and worried Mr Gringle behind them.

'It serves him right,' said Julian. 'To think that he could make that poor little woman slave for him, and never even notice how frightened and unhappy she was – or even see that she had a black eye from that horrible son. Let him get back to his butterflies!'

'What did Mrs Janes mean – mumbling about men hidden in that room – *four* of them she said,' wondered Anne. 'And why did they go and watch on the hillside? What *for*? That must have been one of them you saw that night of the storm, Julian – the one you spotted with the butterfly net, who said he was Mr Brent. I suppose he pretended to be him, so that nobody would ask him why he was prowling out there!'

'Yes, you're right,' said Julian. 'Of course, they may have been watching the airfield, you know – yes, of course that's what they *were* doing! Why didn't I think of that before? They were watching it night and day – two by day, I suppose, and two by night – and paid Janes to keep them hidden in that room. What were they up to?'

'Julian – could it – could it *possibly* be anything to do with the stolen aeroplanes?' asked George, with sudden excitement in her voice.

'It might. It certainly might,' said Julian. 'But I don't know how it ties up with Jeff Thomas and Ray Wells flying them away. That doesn't seem to fit somehow. You know – I really think we're on to something here! Let's go down to Billycock Farm and see if Mr Thomas, Toby's dad, is about. I think we ought to tell him all we know.'

'Yes, that's a good idea,' said Anne, pleased. 'We do want a bit of help over this now.'

'Well, come on then,' said Julian, and off they went at top speed down the hill, taking the path to Billycock Farm. They soon came to the farmyard and called Toby.

'Toby! Where are you? We've got a bit of news.'

Toby appeared at the barn door, looking rather pale, for he'd had a bad night. 'Oh, hello – what news? The only news *I* want to hear is about Jeff. I can't get it out of my mind.'

'Where's your dad?' asked Julian. 'We think he ought to hear what we've got to say. He'll know what to do. I'm afraid we don't – it's a puzzle we can't seem to fit together!'

'I'll call Dad,' said Toby at once, and sent a shout over the field where red-and-white cows were grazing. 'Da-ad! Da-ad! You're WANTED!'

His father came hurrying over the field. 'What is it? I'm busy.'

'Dad – Julian and Dick have got something to tell you,' said Toby. 'It won't take very long – but they're a bit worried.'

'Oh – well, what is it, lads?' said Mr Thomas, turning his kindly brown face to the boys. 'Got into any trouble?'

'Oh no, not exactly,' said Julian. 'I'll tell you as shortly as I can.' And he began to tell him the tale of the butterfly farm – and of the man he had seen at night on the hill – of the old woman at the butterfly farm, and of Will Janes, who treated her so badly. The farmer nodded at that.

'Ay!' he said. 'Will's changed this last year. Got into bad company, of course.'

'We've met some of the "bad company",' said Julian and told of their adventure the night before – and then ended by telling Mr Thomas what the old woman had said to them that morning.

'*Now* what has Will Janes been up to?' said the farmer. 'Bad enough to get into ill company – but worse to ill-treat his poor old mum! He'll have to say who these men are that he's been harbouring up there at the butterfly farm – and why they go out at night – watching the airfield, as you say, I don't doubt. Maybe they've even had a hand in the stealing of those planes!'

Toby became very excited at this and his face grew crimson. 'Dad! Maybe it was those men who took the planes! There were *four*, weren't there? They'd be strong enough to capture Jeff and Ray and take them off somewhere – and then two of them could fly off the planes, and the other two watch poor Jeff and Ray, wherever they are!'

'You know – you may be right, Toby,' said his

father. 'This is a matter for the police – and at once, too. They must get on to Will, and get everything out of him – make him confess. If Jeff and Ray are held prisoner anywhere, they must be freed.'

Toby was dancing round in excitement. 'I *knew* it wasn't Jeff! I knew he couldn't do a thing like that! I'm sure it was two of those men. Dad, get on to the police at once.'

Mr Thomas hurried indoors to the phone, and was soon telling the police all he knew. They listened in astonishment, and at once saw the tremendous importance of the information the children had given.

'We'll question Will Janes at once,' they said. 'He's held on a matter of thieving, so we've got him under our thumb. We'll call you back in about half an hour.'

That half hour was the very longest the children had ever known. Julian looked at his watch dozens of times and nobody could sit still, least of all Toby. Anne was fidgety, and thought she would play with Benny. But neither Benny nor the piglet was there, so she had to wait in patience.

When the phone at last shrilled out everyone

jumped violently. Mr Thomas ran to it. 'Yes – yes – that's the police speaking, is it? Yes, I'm listening. What's the news? Oh . . . yes . . . yes . . .'

The farmer held the phone close to his ear, nodding as he listened intently. The children watched him just as intently, trying to glean something from his few words, and from his face.

'I see. Well – that's very disappointing,' they heard Mr Thomas say, and their hearts sank. 'Thank you. Yes, very worrying indeed. Goodbye!'

He put down the phone and faced the children. Toby called out to him. 'Was it Jeff who stole the plane, Dad? Was it?'

'No!' said his father, and Toby gave a wild yell of joy, and leapt into the air.

'Then nothing else matters!' he cried. 'Oh I *knew* it wasn't Jeff!'

'Wait a minute, wait a minute,' said Mr Thomas. 'There's something very worrying.'

'What?' said Toby, startled.

'Will Janes has confessed that those four men were sent to steal those two planes,' he said. 'Two of them were first-class pilots – foreign. The other two were thugs –sent to capture Jeff and Ray that night in the storm. They knocked them out and dragged them away from the airfield, and hid them somewhere. Then the pilots got out the two planes, and flew away. When the alarm was raised, it was too late.'

'So – when the planes crashed into the sea, it was the *foreign* pilots who were drowned, not Jeff and Ray?' said Julian.

'Yes. But here's the worrying part. The other two men, the ones who captured Jeff and Ray, have hidden them away, but didn't tell Janes *where*!' said Mr Thomas. 'They refused to pay him any money for his help, because the planes had crashed and their plans had failed – and they also refused to tell him where Jeff and Ray were hidden . . .'

'And now I suppose the two thugs have left the district – made their escape – and left Jeff and Ray to starve in some place where they may never be found!' said Toby, sitting down heavily and looking suddenly subdued.

'Exactly,' said Mr Thomas. 'And unless we find out where they are pretty quickly, things will go badly for them – they're probably bound hand and foot – and are dependent on the two for food and water. Once the men are gone, there's no one to bring them anything!'

'Oh no!' said Toby, horrified. 'Dad, we must find them, we *must*!'

'That's what the police think,' said his father. 'And what I think, too. But nobody knows where to look!'

'Nobody knows where to look!' The words repeated themselves in everyone's mind. Nobody knows where to look!

19 *A morning of work*

There was a dead silence after Mr Thomas had said those despairing words – 'Nobody knows where to look!' Where *were* Jeff and Ray lying, worried and anxious, knowing their planes to be stolen, picturing them in the hands of an alien country, being dismantled to discover the new and secret devices built into them!

'They must be absolutely furious to think how easily it was all done!' said Dick. 'Taken by surprise like that! Surely there must be someone on the airfield who was in on the secret?'

'Bound to be,' said Mr Thomas. 'These things are carefully planned to the very last detail – and, of course, it was a bit of luck for the men to have a storm going on just at the time when they needed something to make their getaway unseen and unheard – unheard, that is, until the planes were actually up in the air, and then it didn't matter!'

'Yes – the rain poured down that night,'

said George, remembering. 'Nobody would be out in it – even the guards on the airfield would be under shelter somewhere. It was a bit of luck for those men!'

'I expect they were delighted to look out of the tiny little window at the cottage and see a storm blowing up on the very night they wanted one!' said Dick.

'It beats me how Mr Gringle and Mr Brent never heard or suspected anything – with four strange men hanging about the butterfly farm,' said Julian.

'There can't be *anything* in their heads but butterflies or moths,' said Toby. 'I bet the police will have something to say to *them*!'

'The thing is – what's to be done now?' said Julian, frowning. He turned to Mr Thomas, who was deep in thought. 'What do *you* think? Is there anything we can do?'

'I doubt it,' said Mr Thomas. 'The police have had reports of two men driving a van at a high speed – the number was taken by two or three people who complained – and they think that it might have been the one used to transport Jeff and Ray to some distant hiding place – somewhere in a disused quarry – or in some deserted cellar. Likely places of that sort.'

Everyone groaned. There really was absolutely nothing they could do, then – it would be impossible to hunt for miles for old quarries or other hiding places!

'Well – I must get on with my work,' said Mr Thomas. 'Where's your mum, Toby? You'd better tell her about all this.'

'She's gone shopping,' said Toby, looking at the clock. 'She'll be back just before dinner-time.'

'I suppose Benny has gone with her,' said Mr Thomas, going to the door. 'Where's Curly, his piglet? Surely he hasn't taken him, too!'

'I expect he has,' said Toby. He looked at the other four children, suddenly remembering something. 'Hey – aren't you a bit short of food up at the camp? Shall I get you some to take back with you?'

'Well – if it isn't too much trouble,' said Julian, apologetically. It seemed rather dreadful to think about food when probably Jeff and Ray were lying tied up somewhere, hungry and thirsty, with no chance of food of any sort.

'I'll get some. You come with me, Anne, and

say what you want,' said Toby, and he and Anne went off together to the kitchen, and opened the door of the immense larder. Soon Anne was choosing what she wanted, trying to cheer up poor, downcast Toby at the same time.

'Can we stay and help you this morning, Toby?' asked Julian, when he and Anne came back. He knew that Toby had many jobs to do on the farm, although it was a holiday week – and he thought, too, that it would be good for the boy to have company that worrying morning.

'Yes. I'd like you to!' said Toby, brightening at once. 'I told Dad I'd limewash the hen-houses today – it's just the kind of day for that, nice and dry with a little breeze. You and Dick could help and we'd get them all done by dinner-time.'

'Right. We'll help you all morning, then we'll go back to our camp and have a picnic lunch,' said Julian. 'If you've finished all the jobs you have to do, you could come back with us – and we could go on a hike or something this afternoon.'

'Oh *yes*!' said Toby, cheering up considerably. 'Come on, then – we'll get the lime and find the brushes. Hey Binky, come and help us – and you, too, Timmy.'

'Wait a minute – can't *we* help?' said George. 'I can limewash hen-houses as well as anyone!'

'What about doing a job for my mum instead? She never has time to weed her flower-garden and she's always upset because it's so untidy. Could you and Anne do something about that?'

'Yes!' called Anne, going out of the door. 'Let's find a trowel each, and something to put weeds in. Let's weed the whole bed and make it look good for Mrs Thomas. She's so kind and generous, I'd like to do something for her.'

'All right. So would I,' said George, and went with her cousin into the garden.

'I wish little Benny was at home,' said Anne, as she and George began their task a few minutes later, complete with trowels and two old tin buckets for the weeds. 'I'd like him running round us, asking questions in that little high voice of his. And Curly, his piglet, running about like a funny little pig-puppy!'

'Yes. I like Benny, too,' said George, pulling up a handful of weeds. 'Honestly – there are more weeds than flowers in this bed.'

'Let's take Benny up to the camp with us this

afternoon, if Toby comes,' said Anne. 'Then Toby can take him back with him when he goes. I love little Benny – I could look after him while you and the boys go hiking this afternoon.'

'All right,' said George, torn between wanting to stay with Anne and little Benny and his pig and going with the boys. 'Help – I've been stung by a *vicious* nettle!'

All the children worked hard that morning. The hen-houses had been scrubbed down and well and truly limewashed. Now they were drying quickly, the doors flung open to sun and wind. The girls had practically cleared the big flower-bed of weeds and were feeling rather pleased with it – and with themselves too!

There came the sound of a car at about a quarter to one. 'That must be Mrs Thomas coming back from her shopping,' said George. 'Quick, let's finish this bed before she sees us – there's only about ten minutes' more work.'

'Benny will soon come running to see what we're doing,' said Anne. 'And little Curly, too. Look – I've just filled my ninth bucket of weeds!'

The three boys came by just then, swinging their empty buckets and carrying their big brushes.

Timmy came, too, with quite a few white patches on his coat!

'Hello, girls!' said Dick. 'Hey, you've done a great job on that bed – you can actually see the flowers now!'

The girls sat back pleased. 'Yes, it looks a bit better,' said Anne, pushing back her hair. 'Your mum's home, I think, Toby. We'd better go now, because you'll soon be having your dinner, and we'll be as hungry as hunters by the time we get back to our camp.'

'Right,' said Toby. 'Here, I'll take those buckets of weeds for you – and the trowels!'

'Oh – thanks,' said George. 'Dick, Anne and I will go off to the camp now, with Timmy, and take the salad and stuff that wants washing under the spring – you bring the rest of the food, will you?'

'Of course,' said Dick. 'You take one basket, and we'll take the other.'

They went off with Toby. Anne and George went to look for Mrs Thomas, but she had gone into the dairy and was not to be seen.

'Never mind – she'll be busy,' said Anne. 'We'll go off straight away and get our lunch ready.'

They went off to the farm gate and up the path on to the steep slopes of Billycock Hill, the basket between them. Soon they were out of sight.

The boys washed their hands under a pump in the yard. Toby had gone to see his mother and to tell her what the police had said – but his father had already told her. She was very worried indeed.

'Poor Jeff! Poor Ray!' she said. Then she looked round as she heard the footsteps of Dick and Julian. 'Oh,' she said, 'I thought it was Benny. Where is he?'

'Benny – well, he was with you, wasn't he?' said Toby. 'You didn't leave him in the car, did you?'

'What do you mean, Toby?' said Mrs Thomas, looking startled. 'I left Benny here at the farm. I didn't take him with me – I never do when I have a lot of shopping, he gets so bored!'

'But Mum – I haven't seen him all morning!' said Toby. 'He's not at the farm. I haven't seen him for *hours*!'

'Oh, *Toby*!' said his mother, looking frightened. 'Toby, what's happened to him then? I thought you'd look after him, as you usually do!'

'And I thought he'd gone with *you*,' groaned Toby. 'Dick, Julian – have you seen Benny, or Curly?'

'No – we haven't set eyes on him this morning!' said Dick. 'Where's he got to? He may have gone up Billycock Hill to try and find our camp – I know he wanted to.'

'Toby – the horse-pond!' said Mrs Thomas, looking pale. 'Go there – he may have fallen in. Look in the loft of the barn, too – and go into the machinery shed. Oh, Benny, Benny, where are you?'

She turned to Dick and Julian, standing anxiously beside her. 'Go up to your camp,' she said. 'Hunt and call all the way. He may be lost on the hillside. My little Benny! Perhaps his piglet "runned away" again as he so often tells us – and he followed and got lost! Oh, no, what shall I do?'

20 *A strange message*

Toby raced off to the horse-pond, very frightened. The pond was deep in the middle and Benny couldn't swim. Dick and Julian went off hurriedly through the farm gate and up to Billycock Hill, calling as they went.

'Benny! Benny, where are you? Benny!'

They toiled up the steep, heathery slopes, looking for any sign of the small boy, but there was none. They were both anxious. Benny was such a little wanderer and his pig made such a good excuse for going long distances!

'Benny! BENNY!' they called, and sometimes the echo came back to them, calling the name too.

'Perhaps he'll be at the camp,' said Dick. 'I know he wanted to visit it. He *may* be there, the little monkey – with Curly, too.'

'I hope so,' said Julian, soberly. 'But it's a long way for his small legs to go. I don't see how he could possibly find the way without someone to guide him – he's never been there yet!'

'Well, maybe the girls spotted him on their way up,' said Dick. 'This is quite a day, isn't it? – nobody knows where Jeff and Ray are – and nobody knows where little Benny is either – I don't call this a very good holiday!'

'Exciting – but very worrying,' said Julian. 'Why do we always run into something like this? We *never* seem to have a really peaceful time!'

Dick glanced sideways at Julian and gave a fleeting smile. 'Would you *like* a really peaceful time, Ju?' he said. 'I don't think you would! Come on – let's shout again!'

They came to the camp at last, not having seen a sign of Benny or the piglet. He wasn't at the camp either, that was obvious. The girls and Timmy were alone.

They were horrified when they were told about Benny. Anne went pale.

'Let's go and look for him at once,' she said. 'We must!'

'Well, let's make some sandwiches very quickly?' asked Dick. 'We're all hungry, and it won't take a minute. We can munch them as we go. And let's make a plan of campaign.'

They set to work with the sandwiches. Anne's fingers were all thumbs, she was so shocked to hear that little Benny was missing. 'Oh, I hope nothing's happened to him!' she said. 'Missing all the morning – for hours! Poor Mrs Thomas!'

'Now, what's the plan, Julian?' said George. 'We all separate, I suppose, and search the hill, shouting all the time?'

'That's it,' said Julian, beginning on his sandwiches hungrily, and slipping some tomatoes and radishes into his pocket. 'You go round that side, Anne and George, one of you high up on the hill, and one lower down, so that your shouts cover as much distance as possible. And Dick and I will do the same on this side. We'll go down to the butterfly farm too, in case he's wandered there.'

They all set off, and soon the hill echoed to loud shouts. 'BENNY! BE-ENNY! BENNY! Coo-ee Benny! Coo-ee!'

Over the heather scrambled the four, with Timmy excitedly leaping about, too. He knew that Benny was lost, and he was sniffing for some smell of the small boy – but his sharp nose could find nothing.

Julian went to the butterfly farm and searched all about, but there was no sign of the boy there. In fact there was no sign of anyone, not even Mrs Janes. She had gone off somewhere, and the two men were out butterflying as usual. In fact, George and Anne saw them as they searched their side of the hill and called to them.

'Have you seen anything of a small boy and a little pig?'

The two men were curt and unhelpful. 'No. No sign at all.'

'I suppose they're annoyed because they still think the boys broke the glass of their butterfly house!' said George. 'Well, I wish they'd hunt for Benny instead of butterflies.'

It was two hours before Benny was found, and the Five had almost given up looking for him. They had met together as they came round the hill, and were standing in despair, wondering what to do next, when Timmy suddenly pricked up his ears. Then he barked – an excited little bark that said as clearly as possible, 'I've heard something interesting.'

'What is it then, Tim, what is it?' cried George

at once. 'Go find, go find!'

Timmy trotted off, his ears well pricked up. He stopped every now and again and listened, then went on again. The children listened, too, but they could hear nothing – no call, no groan, no whimper.

'He's going downhill towards the caves,' said Julian at last. '*The caves*! Why didn't we think of those? But how could that tiny little boy have found the way there? It's a long and complicated way from Billycock Farm.'

'He might have followed Curly, the pig,' said Anne. 'We always thought that he only *pretended* that the pig ran away, so that he could wander where he liked and blame it on the pig. But this time the pig might *really* have "runned away"!'

'Let's hope it's Benny that Timmy can hear,' said Julian. 'I can't hear a single sound and I've got pretty sharp ears!'

And then the next minute they *all* heard something – a small, tired voice calling high and clear – 'Curly! Curly! I want you!'

'BENNY!' yelled everyone and leapt ahead so fast that the heathery ground shook beneath their trampling feet.

Timmy was there first, of course, and when the four children came up, they saw him gently licking the golden-haired little boy, who had put his arms round the dog's neck in delight. Benny was sitting just outside the entrance of the caves, all by himself – his piglet wasn't there.

'Benny! Oh, Benny, we've found you,' cried Anne, and knelt down beside him. He looked up at the others, not seeming at all surprised to see them.

'Curly runned away,' he said. 'He runned *right* away. Curly went in there,' and he pointed into the caves.

'Thank goodness you didn't follow him!' said George. 'You might never have been found! Come along – we must take you home!'

But as soon as she lifted up the child he began to kick and scream. 'No! No! I want Curly! I want Curly!'

'Benny, he'll come along when he's tired of the caves,' said Anne. 'But your mummy wants you now – and your dinner's waiting for you.'

'I'm hungry,' announced Benny. 'I want my dinner – but I want Curly, too. Curly! Curly! Come here!'

'We *must* take Benny back,' said Dick. 'His mum will be so worried. Curly will eventually come out if he's got sense enough to remember the way – if not well – it's just too bad! We daren't go wandering down the unroped paths in case we get lost. Come on, bring Benny, George.'

'Curly will come when he's ready,' George said, as she carried the little boy away from the entrance to the caves. 'But now your mummy wants you, and your dinner's waiting.'

With Timmy jumping up delightedly beside her, she carried the small boy down the chalky path, talking to him. They were all so thankful to have found him that they felt quite cheerful, forgetting Jeff and Ray for a while. They teased little Benny playfully, trying to make him forget his lost pet.

Mrs Thomas was overjoyed to see the small boy again. She cried over him as she took him into her arms. 'Oh, Benny, Benny – what a bad pair you are, you and your piglet.'

'He runned away,' said Benny, of course.

He was set down at the table to have his dinner and began to eat very fast indeed because he was so hungry. Everyone sat and watched him, so glad to have him safe again that they hardly took their eyes off him while he gobbled his meal.

He finished at last. 'I'm going to look for Curly,' he announced as he got down from his chair.

'Oh, no, you're not,' said his mother. 'You're going to stay with me. I want you to help me to make some cakes. Curly will come home when he's ready.'

And in an hour's time, when Julian, Dick, Anne, George and Toby were busy at the messy job of cleaning out the duck-pond, Curly did come back. He trotted into the farmyard, making his usual funny little squeals, and everyone looked round at once.

'CURLY! You *have* come back! Oh, you bad little pig!' cried George, and Timmy ran up to the piglet and sniffed him and licked him. The pig turned himself round to look for Benny – and Julian laughed.

'Someone's written something on him – in black! Come here, Curly, and let's see.'

Curly trotted over to him, and Julian examined the rather smudged black lettering. 'Can't make it out,' he said. 'Somebody's printed something on his pink little body – silly thing to do – but it'll wash off.'

'Wait!' said Dick sharply, as Julian bent to get one of the rags they were using, to wash the piglet's body. 'WAIT! Look – isn't that a J and a T and below those are letters that look like R and V – no, W, because half that letter has been rubbed off by the heather or something.'

Now everyone was staring in excitement. 'J . . . T, and R . . . W!' said Toby in a breathless voice. Then it rose to a shout. 'They stand for JEFF THOMAS AND RAY WELLS. What does it *mean* – who put those letters there?'

'There are some more letters, smaller and rather smudged,' said Julian. 'Hold the piglet still, Dick. We must, we *must* make out what they are! It's some kind of message from Jeff and Ray. The piglet must have been where they're hidden!'

They all looked earnestly at the smudgy letters, which appeared to be five in number. They were almost unreadable – but Dick's sharp brain got hold of them at last.

'The word is CAVES!' he said. 'See – the first letter might be G or O or C – but the third one is definitely V and the last is S. I'm sure it's CAVES – and that's where Curly went, we know.'

'That's where Jeff and Ray are hidden then,'

said Julian. 'Quite near, after all – and we thought they'd been taken away by car and hidden miles away! Quick – where's your dad, Toby?'

Mr Thomas was found and was shown Curly, with the smudgy black letters on his back. He was astounded. 'So Curly went wandering in the caves, did he – what a pig he is! Can't keep his nose out of anything! And somehow he went to where Jeff and Ray were. What a strange way to send a message – they could surely have tied one on to his tail, or round his neck – these letters are almost unreadable!'

'I nearly washed them off, thinking that somebody had played a silly joke on Curly,' said Julian. 'If I had, we wouldn't have known where Jeff and Ray were. What shall we do now? Go to the caves at once? Phone the police?'

'Both!' said Mr Thomas. 'The police have to know because they're searching everywhere, of course. Now – you start off to the caves – but take a ball of string with you, because Jeff and Ray won't have been hidden in any of the roped tunnels, where sightseers so often go, and without string you might not be able to find your way back down the unroped ones. You may find that you need to unwind the string in order to get back safely. And take Timmy. He'll be useful.'

'He certainly will!' said Julian. 'And we'll take the little pig, too, so that Timmy can smell him, and then smell the tracks Curly made as he wandered through the caves, and follow them! We won't have to wander all about wondering where Jeff and Ray are then.'

The Five set off at once, with Toby, too, all as excited as they could possibly be.

'Good old Jeff! Good old Ray!' Toby kept saying. 'We're coming! Hang on, we're coming!'

21 *An exciting finish*

Up the heathery hill panted the five children and Timmy. Julian carried the frightened little pig, who wasn't at all sure what was happening to him. He kicked and squealed but nobody took any notice of him – he would be of importance when they reached the caves, but not till then!

At last they reached the chalky roadway to the caves and pounded along it, the loose bits of chalk flying between their feet. They came to the entrance where the warning notice stood.

'Timmy!' called George as Julian put down the trembling little pig and held him tightly. 'Timmy – come here! Smell Curly – that's right – smell him all over – now follow, follow, follow! Smell where he went in the caves – and follow, Tim, follow!'

Timmy knew perfectly well what tracking meant and obediently smelt Curly thoroughly, and then put his nose to the ground to follow the scent of the piglet's footsteps. He soon picked it up, and began to run into the first cave.

He stopped and looked back enquiringly. 'Go on, Tim, go on – I know this seems strange to you when we've got Curly here – but we want to know where he *went*!' called George, afraid that Timmy might think it was just a silly game and give up. Timmy put his nose to the ground again.

He came to the magnificent cave, full of gleaming 'icicles', the stalactites and stalagmites, some of them looking like shining pillars. Then into the next cave, which, with its glowing rainbow colours, had reminded Anne of a Fairyland cave. Then through the next cave they went – and came to the forking of the ways.

'Here we are – at the three tunnels,' said George. 'I bet Timmy won't go down the usual roped one that all visitors would take . . .'

As she spoke the words Timmy, nose to ground, still following the scent of the piglet's footsteps, took the left-hand, unroped way – and everyone followed, torches shining brightly.

'I thought so!' said George, and her voice began to echo around. 'Thought so, thought so, so, so . . . !'

'Do you remember those awful noises we heard the other day – that piercing whistling, and those howls?' said Dick. 'Well, I bet they were made by the bullies who dragged Jeff and Ray here! I expect they heard Timmy barking – *he* must have heard the men, probably, although we didn't – and they were scared in case we were coming. So they made those horrible noises to scare us off, and the echoes magnified them.'

'Well, they certainly scared us away all right,' said Anne, remembering. 'Yes – it must have been those men – there aren't any awful noises today! What a long, winding tunnel this is – and look, it's forking into two!'

'Timmy will know which way to take,' said George – and, of course he did. With his nose to the ground, he chose the left-hand one without any hesitation.

'You didn't really need to bring a ball of string, Julian,' said Toby. 'Timmy will easily be able to take us the right way back, won't he?'

'Yes,' said Julian. 'He's better than any unwinding ball of string! But without Tim we'd *never* find the way back – there are so many caves, and so many tunnels. We must be well into the heart of the hill now.'

Timmy suddenly stopped in his tracking, raised his head, and listened. Could he hear Jeff and Ray? He barked loudly – and from somewhere in the near distance came a shout. 'Hoy! Hoy! This way! This way!'

'It's Jeff!' shouted Toby, dancing in the dark tunnel with excitement. 'JEFF! CAN YOU HEAR ME? JEFF!'

And a voice came back at once. 'Hi, Toby! This way, this way!'

Timmy ran down the passage and stopped. At first the children couldn't see why – and then they saw that the passage came to an end there – a blank wall faced them just beyond Timmy – and yet Jeff's voice came very clearly to them!

'Here we are, here!'

'There's a hole in the floor of the tunnel just by Timmy!' cried Julian, shining his torch on it. 'That's where Jeff and Ray are – down that hole. Hey, Jeff – are you down there?'

Julian shone his torch right through the hole – and there, lying on the floor of a cave below was Ray – and standing beside him, looking up eagerly, was Jeff!

'You've found us!' he said. 'Those men told us they were leaving us here and not coming back. Ray's got a twisted ankle – he can't stand on it. They pushed us down this hole without any warning, and he fell awkwardly. But with your help we can get him up.'

'Jeff, oh, Jeff – I'm so glad we've found you!' yelled Toby, trying to look down into the hole with Julian. 'What's the best way to get you up? This entrance hole isn't very big.'

'If you can manage to pull *me* up, that's the first thing to do,' said Jeff, considering the matter. 'Then two of you can go down to Ray, and help him to stand, and I think I could haul *him* up. This is an awful place – no outlet except through that small hole up there, which was too high for me to jump up to – and Ray couldn't stand, of course, to help me!'

There was soon a great deal of acrobatic work on the part of Jeff, Julian and Dick! The two boys managed to haul up Jeff by lying down on the floor above, and putting their arms and shoulders through the hole to drag him up! Toby and George had to hold on to their legs to prevent them from being pulled into the hole! And Anne had to hold the little pig, which did its best to try and get down the hole, too!

At last Jeff was up through the hole, and then the two boys, Julian and Dick, leapt down to Ray. He seemed rather dazed and Jeff said that he thought he had hurt his head as well as his leg when the men pushed them down the hole. Julian pulled him gently to his feet and then he and Dick lifted him until he could reach Jeff's swinging hands as he leaned down through the hole.

Poor Ray was pulled up at last, and then up went Julian and Dick in the same way. Timmy thought the whole procedure was extraordinary, and produced volleys of excited barks, scaring the little pig almost out of its skin!

'Phew!' said Jeff, when at last Ray was up, and being helped by the others. 'I never thought we'd get out of there. Let's get away from this nightmare place as quickly as possible. What we want is a little fresh air and food – *and* water! Those thugs haven't been near us for what seems like weeks!'

They made their way back to the cave entrance, Timmy leading the way confidently, not even troubling to smell it. He never forgot a path once he'd been along it.

They came out into the bright June sunshine, and it was so very dazzling to the two men who had been so long in pitch-black darkness that they had to shade their eyes.

'Sit down a bit till you get used to it,' said Julian. 'And tell us how you wrote your message on the pig! Did he suddenly appear down the hole?'

Jeff laughed. 'Well,' he said, 'there we were down in that awful hole, Ray and I – with no watch to tell us the time, no means of knowing if it was night or day, or even if it was last Thursday or next Monday! And suddenly we heard a pitter-pattering noise – and the next thing we knew was that something had fallen down through the hole and landed on top of us! It began to squeal like mad, so we guessed it was a little pig – although why a pig would suddenly descend on us out of the dark tunnel above us we just couldn't think!'

Everyone laughed, even Ray. 'Go on,' said Dick. 'What did you do?'

'Well, we felt the pig all over and knew it was a baby,' said Jeff, 'but it didn't occur to us for some time that we might use it as a messenger! That was Ray's bright idea!'

'We could hardly read your message,' said Dick. 'It was just touch and go that we made it out.'

'I daresay – but when you consider that we'd been robbed of everything – even my pencil and pen – to say nothing of my money, my watch and my torch – and Ray's, too – and that it was pitch-dark in the hole, I'm sure you'll agree that we didn't make a bad job of printing that message!' said Jeff.

'But what did you print it with if your pockets had been emptied?' asked George, in wonder.

'Well, Ray found a tiny bit of black chalk at the bottom of his trouser pocket,' said Jeff. 'It's chalk we use to mark out our air-routes, on big maps – and that was all we had to use! Ray held the piglet and I printed our initials and the word CAVES on his back. I couldn't see what I was doing in the dark, but I just hoped for the best. Then I stood up and threw the poor little pig through the hole! It was a pretty good shot – I heard him scrambling on the edge, and then away he trotted, the best little pig in the world!'

'What a tale!' said Julian. 'You're lucky, Jeff, that the piglet came home all right! It's a wanderer, that pig, always running away. And to think that

I nearly washed your message off his back before we read it.'

'It gives me the creeps to hear that,' said Jeff. 'Now tell me what happened when it was discovered that we'd disappeared from the airfield – was there a fuss?'

'For sure! You knew your planes were stolen didn't you?' said Dick.

'I guessed that, when I heard two planes take off, just as some great thugs were hauling us up the hill,' said Jeff. 'I heard a dog barking as we were being kicked and dragged up – was it Timmy? I did hope he'd come to our rescue.'

'Oh, *yes* – that must have been the time when he began to bark that night of the storm!' said George, remembering. 'So it was you and those thugs he heard – oh, what a pity we didn't know it!'

'Those two stolen planes crashed into the sea during the storm, Jeff,' said Toby. 'The pilots weren't found.'

'Oh,' said Jeff and was silent for a moment. 'I'll miss my old plane – well let's hope I get another one – and Ray, too. Ray! How do you feel now? Can you hobble along again or not?'

'Yes – if the boys can help me as they did just now,' said Ray, who was already looking much better since he had been in the open air. 'Let's get along.'

It was very slow going – but fortunately the police met them halfway, on their way to the caves! Mr Thomas had phoned them and they had come along immediately. They took Ray in hand, and the little group made better progress.

'Put that pig down, Anne, you must be tired of carrying it,' said Dick. 'You look like Alice in Wonderland. She carried a pig, too!'

Anne laughed. 'I think it's gone to sleep, just like Alice's pig!' she said. And so it had!

They were all very thankful when at last they arrived at Billycock Farm. What a welcome they had from Mrs Thomas, her husband and Benny. The little boy dragged his piglet from Anne's arms and hugged it. 'You runned away, you're bad, you runned fast!' he scolded, and set it down. It immediately scampered over to the barn, with Benny in pursuit and Anne went to fetch them back.

'Now we'll all have tea – I've got it ready, hoping that everyone would be back in time from their adventures!' said Mrs Thomas. 'I know Jeff and Ray must be starved – you look quite thin in the face, Jeff.'

They all sat round the big table, Toby next to his hero, Cousin Jeff. They gazed with pleasure at the food there – surely never, never had there been such a spread before!

'Mum!' said Toby, his eyes gleaming. 'Mum, this isn't a meal – it's a BANQUET! Jeff – what will you have?'

'Everything!' said Jeff. 'Some of every single thing. I'll start with two boiled eggs, three slices of ham, two thick pieces of bread and butter, and some of that wonderful salad. It's almost worth being down that hole for ages to end up with a feast like this!'

It was a really hilarious tea, and for once Benny sat at the table throughout the whole meal, and didn't slip from his chair to go and find Curly. Why didn't they have parties like this every day? Even his father was there, roaring with laughter! What a pity the two policemen hadn't been able to stay for tea, too – Benny had a lot of questions to ask policemen! Where was Timmy? Yes, he was under the table – Benny could feel him with his foot. And, yes, Binky was there, too, just by Toby.

He slid his hand down with a large piece of cake in it, and immediately it was taken gently from his hand by a hairy mouth – Timmy was having a wonderful time, too!

Everyone was sorry when the wonderful meal was over. Jeff and Ray now had to report to the airfield, and Mr Thomas offered to take them in his car. The children went to see them off.

'It'll seem very boring now, up in our camp on the hillside,' said Dick. 'So many things have happened in the last few days – and now nothing will happen at all!'

'Rubbish!' said Jeff. 'I *promise* you something will happen – something wonderful!'

'What?' asked everyone eagerly.

'I'll see that you're all given a free flight in a plane as soon as possible – perhaps tomorrow,' said Jeff. 'And – *I'll* pilot it! Now then – anyone want to loop the loop with me?'

What shouts and squeals from everyone! Jeff made a face and put his hands to his ears.

'Me too, me too – and Curly!' came Benny's little high voice.

'Where *is* Curly?' said Jeff, looking out of the car. 'I really must shake trotters with him – he's been a wonderful friend to me and Ray! Wherever is he?'

'I don't know,' said Benny, looking all around. 'He must have . . .'

'Runned away!' chorused everyone, and Timmy barked at the sudden shout. He put his paws up on the car and licked Jeff's hand.

'Thanks, boy,' said Jeff. 'We couldn't have done without you either! Bye, everybody – see you tomorrow – and then whoooops! – up in the clouds we'll go!'